SVEN THE COLLECTOR

DOKIRI BRIDES SERIES

DENALI DAY

Copyright © 2019 by Denali Day

All rights reserved.

No part of this book may be reproduced in any form or by any electronic or mechanical means, including information storage and retrieval systems, without written permission from the author, Denali Day, except for the use of brief quotations in a book review.

Line editing by Kelley Luna

Copy editing by May Freighter

Cover Design by Covers by Combs

To Sarra Cannon

The "crazy" woman who told me my dreams were possible, and then showed me the way.

CONTENTS

1. Colette	1
2. Sven	14
3. Sven	22
4. Colette	31
5. Colette	42
6. Colette	53
7. Colette	62
8. Colette	73
9. Colette	80
10. Colette	88
Epilogue	91
The Dokiri Brides Series	95
About the Author	97
Acknowledgments	99

1
COLETTE

The summer wind whipped at Colette's sun-kissed face as she drove her mare on toward her quarry. The elusive fox raced through the grove, silver tail bobbing over the tall grass like a shining beacon, beckoning the hounds. Colette suppressed a cry of exhilaration as her mount leapt over a fallen branch and landed without so much as a hitch in its graceful stride. Behind them, Colette's brothers, father, and a dozen of his men struggled to keep pace. As usual.

The hounds howled, igniting a fresh burst of speed in her horse. Colette reached back for her bow; they were almost close enough for a decent shot. The smell of dampened earth and the babbling of a nearby stream sent a wave of frustration pounding through her.

Not now! Just a bit farther!

Ahead, the fox bounded through the grass and slipped into the treeline. *No time.* Colette drew an arrow and loosed it at the woodland creature. The recoil of the bowstring slapped at her leather bracer as the arrow went zooming.

It missed.

Need one more shot. Just one more.

Colette cursed and drove her heels into her horse's sides. Inhaling, she drew another arrow and took aim. She released the bowstring just as the fox took a bounding leap through the brook that bisected her father's lands. The arrowhead missed its target by mere inches, bouncing off a stone that peaked above the water's bubbling surface. Beneath her, Colette felt her horse's body tense, preparing to make the jump. Gulping down a breath, Colette yanked back on the reigns, drawing her horse to a skidding halt just before they reached the water's edge.

For a moment, the sound of her own breath was all she could hear, followed by the puffing of her mare, and the pounding hooves of her huntmates' horses. A handful of riders rushed past, their wind taking strands of coppery hair out of her braid.

Colette sat stiffly in her saddle, stifling the unladylike urge to spit in their wake. *They* suffered no hesitation, flying like birds over the narrow creek bed, kicking up water and landing surefooted on the other side to continue the morning's hunt. How she envied them.

Hollen, her youngest brother, whooped at her from across the stream. The taunt was more than she could take; Colette jabbed her hand in the air, flashing the most obscene gesture she knew. It might have been more impactful if Hollen himself hadn't been the one to teach it to her. His horse rearing back, he laughed before sprinting deeper into the grove after the others.

Bloody swiver.

"Colette. Come, Daughter. We will go around."

Colette swallowed back the bitter taste in her mouth and turned in her saddle toward her father. Lord Potrulis was a portly man whose frequent hunts were all that kept his waistline from matching the rounding of his smile-worn cheeks. Four guards flanked him, although their presence was more for Colette's sake than for her father or brother's. Lord Potrulis' expression softened with the doting warmth he reserved for his only daughter, and Colette had to surrender some of her ire. But there was something else in his manner that morning which Colette couldn't name.

"Looks like Gareth will be making the kill today," she grumbled, tugging the reigns to follow her father up the creekside.

His guards made room for her to take her place at his left, farthest away from the embankment. She was glad for their silence. All of them knew about her irrational fear of water, so no one questioned why they must now make the three-mile detour to the nearest footbridge. They trotted on at a leisurely pace, assured that the fox was well out of reach.

"Or Willam might bring it down," Lord Potrulis said. "That boy's been chomping at the bit for something to present to that new wife of his."

Colette snorted. "I don't think he'll find his way into the new Lady Potrulis' heart with a bloody pelt."

"Ah. But your sister-in-law has an eye for furs."

"Mmm. And other fine things."

Lord Potrulis shot his daughter a mildly reproachful look. "Not every woman can occupy herself with nothing but the hunt for distraction, Daughter."

"Indeed not, Father. There's also riding, archery, falconry, and swordplay." Colette flashed her father her most winning grin, the one that was sure to earn her a laugh and rueful shake of his graying head. She received neither, and she had to ignore the itch tingling at the back of her neck. What was on her father's mind this morning? Perhaps she should kick her mare into a canter before she was made to find out.

She started to do just that when her father caught her mount by the reigns, staying her escape. Colette arched a brow as Lord Potrulis ordered his guards to hang back, allowing some distance between them. Defeated, Colette rode alongside her father, preparing for whatever reproach he was about to give.

"Your mother and I are meeting with Lord Myron tomorrow night. We'd like you to attend with us."

Colette frowned. She didn't care for Lord Myron, and she cared for his simpering heir even less. The younger Myron had a habit of following about on Colette's heels until she could convince one of her older brothers to divert him with some invitation. Of course that, unfortunately, meant Colette had to excuse herself from her brother's revelry if she was to gain any peace. This time would be worse. She'd be going to *him*.

"Will any of my brothers be attending?"

Lord Potrulis shifted awkwardly in his saddle. "No."

Curses. Then she was on her own. She sighed but said nothing, sensing now was not the time to protest. Perhaps she could feign illness at dinner tonight, and thus gain excusal from the journey. Birds in the nearby trees tittered their morning song as shafts of sunlight filtered in through the branches. Closing her eyes, Colette breathed in the dew-set air.

"Colette, dearest..."

Oh no.

Colette's eyes popped open. Nothing good ever came from that endearment. She shifted a sidelong glance at her father who was peering intently at her. The urge to bolt once again took hold, and Colette's mare nickered in response to the tension rising in her body.

"You know your mother and I only want what's best for you."

No. No. No.

If her father was invoking her mother's name, then she was guaranteed not to like whatever came next. Forcing a smile, Colette nodded at her fidgeting father.

"And after a lot of thought and"—he scratched at his beard,

appearing to struggle for the right words—"more than enough time, we've decided it might be best for you to...to..."

Don't say it.

"To marry."

Swiving hell.

Colette fluttered her lashes at her father as though confused. "Marry? Father, what do you mean?"

Lord Potrulis' face flushed, and he went back to scratching his beard. Were she not so mortified, she could have embraced her father for his timidity. In general, Lord Potrulis loathed upsetting his cherished daughter, and no doubt he was only broaching this subject now because his wife had demanded he does so. Colette's mother had long ago ceased trying to reason with her unruly daughter. The day had come none too soon for Colette, who shared so little in common with her prim and proper mother, the picture of all that a Morhageese noblewoman should be. When her father spoke again, she could almost hear her mother's voice coming out of his mouth.

"This should come as no surprise to you, Colette. You've twenty-one years behind you, far more than any other unmarried women of your station."

"Lady Evangeline Ellis is yet unmarried, and she's twenty-five."

"Lady Ellis has a bastard son. I don't care what your mother says. Your reputation can't be so spoiled as that."

The reputation he referred to was that of any woman who had the audacity to engage in diversions outside of fan waving and embroidery. Colette had bid her reputation farewell many years ago with a cheer of 'good riddance'. After all, what could she do with a reputation? With a liability like that about her neck, her mother would have had her married off long ago.

"Are you certain, Father? I should think you burdened to find me an obliging husband, what with all my drinking, gambling and"—she dropped her voice to a conspiratory whisper—"*damn* profanity."

Despite his unease, Lord Potrulis flashed his daughter an indulgent grin. For all the efforts her mother had put forth to ensure she raised a proper lady, Lord Potrulis had managed to benignly undermine them with his blatant approval of Colette's rougher nature. When called out for his contribution to the tomboy that was their daughter, Lord Potrulis was quick to blame the influence of his five older sons, but the truth was plain: Lord Potrulis adored Colette precisely the way she was and would do nothing to change her.

Until now, it seemed.

His smile faded. "Daughter, the young Lord Myron has asked for your hand."

Colette's mouth dropped in feigned shock. "What?"

Lord Potrulis' lips quirked wryly. "Come now, this can't really surprise you. The man adores you."

"Adores me? He'd lick the dirt from the bottom of my shoe!"

"You say that like it's a bad thing."

"Of course it is! Father, he once followed me around at a party begging for a dance no matter how many times I refused him. I finally told him I would after I returned from the privy. The man waited at the door for me until the hostess declared the festivities over."

"So?"

"He waited there for *four* hours, Father."

The lines in Lord Potrulis' brow deepened. "You hid in a privy for four hours?"

"Of course not. I snuck out the window."

For a moment, Colette thought her father was going to laugh. Instead, he pinched the bridge of his nose between his thumb and forefinger. "Your mother was right. You need to settle down. Perhaps marriage will do the trick."

Sven the Collector

"You and mother really think marriage to Lord Myron will tame me? His older sister has but to frown at him, and he cowers in her shadow. What do you think marriage to me will accomplish? Have you no pity for the man?

Her father huffed. "Less than I should, no doubt. But what would you have me do? Is it a strong man you're after? Your mother's first choice was Lord Brandor."

Colette's blood ran cold. Abrasive and surly, Lord Brandor was more than twice Colette's age. Worse, on the two occasions he and Colette had met, he'd eyed her with a sort of crude assessment like he was considering the best way to break a wild horse. If there was one thing Colette feared more than being saddled with a nitwit like Lord Myron, it was the thought of being lashed to a brute like Lord Brandor. A spirit like hers would be wasted on one man and snuffed out by the other.

Reality began to set in and adrenaline sent Colette's heart pounding. Her knuckles blanched as her grip on the reins tightened. "Father, you can't really mean to go through with this."

"I'm afraid I do. I mean, look at you." He batted a hand in Colette's general direction even as he avoided her with his eyes. "You're not a child anymore. Even *you* must have known these days couldn't last forever."

Colette swallowed hard as her mind reached for some way to sidestep this disaster. This could not be happening. Her father had made declarations of an impending change in the past, typically after some minor scandal had been discovered by her mother, and she'd leveled a hysterical tirade upon her poor husband's ears. Little usually came of them. Why should this be any different? She simply had to be clever.

"Father, can we not invite the Myrons to our keep tomorrow instead? There need be no haste in making any arrangement. Perhaps they could even stay the week. I'm certain that, with a bit of time, I could find it within myself to look upon this situation more favorably."

An utter lie. But if Colette could get the young Lord Myron to her family's home, she was certain she could induce her five older brothers to 'reason' him out of his affections for her. The poor lord would probably faint as soon as he found himself alone and at the center of her imposing siblings' attention. At times, there were advantages to being the only daughter in such a large family.

"The arrangements have already been made."

Colette's spine straightened. She drew back on her reigns and swayed with her mount as it shifted irritably from one side to the other.

Lord Potrulis turned his own steed around, glancing back at his daughter. His mouth was pulled into a tight line. "I signed your marriage contract weeks ago. We're taking you to Myron's for the commencement of your engagement."

"You...you already gave me up?"

Her father's jaw slackened, and he extended an open palm toward her. "Now Daughter, don't be that way about it."

Tears welling, Colette drew backward, avoiding his touch. "How could you?"

He sighed, his eyes hardening into what must have been often rehearsed willpower. "I know the life of a lady doesn't excite you, dearest, but the world we live in isn't kind to unmarried women, particularly not to ones as lovely and spirited as you. There will come a day when I'm not around anymore, and your brothers will have their own families and affairs to look after. I want to make sure you're safe. Protected."

"I can protect myself."

Colette knew she sounded like a petulant child, especially as her voice cracked, but she couldn't stop herself. With her father's every word, she could feel her freedom being sucked away and there was nothing she could do to stop it. He'd signed a contract? And he'd waited until now to tell her? To keep her from doing something foolish, no doubt. Damn.

Lord Potrulis smiled sadly. "From a wolf or an unwanted suitor. But there are worse things, things you can't stave off with blade or bow."

She arched her brow in challenge. "Like a life of subjugation?"

"Like a lifetime of solitude and pariahood. As for subjugation, I know you won't give the idea any credit, but you might find that submitting yourself to the right man can bring a measure of satisfaction."

Colette wasn't sure if it was shock or outrage that brought the heat to her cheeks. Her father was resolved, she could see that now. Misery dropped like a sinking stone into the pit of her stomach. Her vision blurred as she stared through her father toward the open pasture ahead.

"Maybe you're right..."

Lord Potrulis sat quietly on his horse, no doubt hoping for his daughter's forgiveness and swift acceptance of her new situation. Beloved as he was, he'd always have the former. The latter? Not a chance.

"But damn me to hell if Lord Myron is *that* man."

With a kick of Colette's heels, her mare shot forward, brushing past her father's nickering steed. She heard her father call and whistle for the guards to hurry in pursuit. She wasn't really running away. Surely they knew that. Where could she go? Still, the instinct to flee was overwhelming, and Colette basked in the glorious sensation of temporarily escaping fate. For a moment, she was the fox, but unlike it, she wouldn't be caught until she was good and resigned to be. Leaning forward, she galloped over the grassy-green plain.

Up ahead, a flash of silver caught Colette's attention. She

squinted against the early climbing sun. *Could it be? Two silver-tails in one hunt?* The tuft of shining fur disappeared then reemerged as the fox leapt around a gray boulder. Despite everything, Colette grinned and urged her horse onward.

They burst through the meadow, picking up speed and lengthening the distance between them and her father's men. Right about now, father was probably cursing himself for gifting her with such a fine steed. Between it and her own considerable skill, catching up with Colette would be a feat. *Splendid.*

They were almost there. The fox had been caught in the open, and the creature had little chance of escaping. It raced up and over a nearby knoll, disappearing over the edge. Cresting the hill, Colette's eyes scanned the dipping valley below. A gust of wind had her batting stray locks of hair out of her face just as she caught sight of her quarry. It was racing down toward the darkened treeline. Colette's breath caught in her throat.

The Twist.

"Hyah!" She drove her heels into her mare's sides, urging her to run faster before it was too late. Reaching back, Colette drew up her bow, determined to make the kill before the fox could vanish into that black labyrinth. Leaning low in the saddle to preserve her balance, she lined up the shot and released her arrow.

The shaft just grazed across the fox's hip, and it yipped. A flash of crimson assured Colette that she'd nicked her target, but the animal did not slow. It sped on, dissolving into the stunted shadows of the trees.

"No!"

This was not how her final hunt as a free woman was going to end. Heedless of the danger, Colette urged her mare forward, ignoring its whinnying protest. Injured, the fox wouldn't last long, and Colette would be damned if she left its fine pelt to rot in the dirt. As she blew past the treeline, the forest's cool shade doused her flesh, and Colette stifled a shiver.

From some distance back, Lord Potrulis shouted in frenzied alarm, begging his daughter to turn back. She ignored him, driving deeper into the outer border of the woods. A thrill of wicked satisfaction made her burst into laughter. Even now, her father was probably praising the gods that her unpredictable nature would soon be some other man's dilemma. Fair enough.

Dodging the blackened trees and leaping over fallen branches, Colette followed the trail of blood. The air had changed, devoid of the scent of grass, blossoms, and other living things. It seemed that even the birds avoided this part of the land, the twisted canopy as silent as the bare ground below it. Colette ignored the tingling sensation at the nape of her neck, reasoning that her instincts couldn't know how briefly she planned to stay. She only needed to reach that fox.

Relief washed over her as she burst through another line of trees and into an open field. The grass was taller here but a dull, russet color. Bright flecks of blood against the pale stalks guided her into the center of the wide clearing until, at last, she could see her fallen quarry. It lay on its side. Slinging her bow across her chest and snatching up a burlap sack, Colette dismounted her sweat-slicked mare and hurried over.

A twinge of sympathy pinched at Colette's gut as she knelt down at the animal's side. Its black eyes found hers, and, for a moment, she could almost feel its pain. Withdrawing her hunting knife, Colette put a swift end to its suffering. It was young and fat, its brown coat glossy even under the shaded sky. Stunning. Her brothers would be envious, indeed. Good. It would serve them right for leaving her behind. With a smirk on her face, Colette stuffed her kill into the sack and stood to call her horse.

With a prickle of surprise, Colette realized that her father and his men had not followed her into the woods. The Twist was said to be home to countless terrors. Few ever ventured within and returned to tell the tale. But it wasn't as if Colette had embarked on some great quest. She'd retrieved her kill and now she would return. The whole affair wouldn't have taken more than twenty minutes. Smugness flared as Colette realized she'd just accomplished something grown men weren't willing to do. Another boast for her haughty brothers.

Pursing her lips, Colette was about to whistle when her mare bolted off in the direction they'd come. Dumbfounded, Colette could only stare. Her mount was raised and trained by the king's own horsemaster and had never been the skittish sort. Squinting, Colette whistled, trying to bring the mare around. A rising sense of dread crept up her throat as the mare, heedless to her mistress's call, continued on and disappeared into the trees.

Had that really just happened? Was she seriously standing alone in the middle of the Twist without a ride? Colette blinked. What in the hells was she going to do now?

Just as she was putting it together that she'd be hiking her stubborn tail back, a blast of wind bent her shoulders downward toward the brittle grass. Though the sun had been hiding behind the clouds, a darker shadow cast onto the ground, surrounding Colette in its chilling embrace. An inner voice, deep and primal, told her what was about to happen, and, before she could think on it, Colette turned her face toward the sky.

Eight ivory talons extended their razor-sharp tips above her. Colette's scream was muffled to her own ears, drowned out by the sound of rushing wind spilling past her face. She dropped to the ground, her only instinct to get away. Before she could roll onto her stomach, she was being scooped up, dragged by the waist into the air. Her free hand sprung open, releasing bits of dirt and torn grass. She twisted her head backward and watched as the debris seemed to float back toward the rapidly departing earth. She screamed again, and, this time, she couldn't hear at all against the gusting howl.

Vertigo, rather than calm, made her cease thrashing long enough to get a look at the creature carrying her. Pale, leathery wings with four long spines beat toward the clouds above. A mosaic of white and gray scales ran the length on a long, slender neck that ended in a head full of spikes and jagged fangs.

Skies, I'm being carried by a dragon!

Could this be real? Was she truly the prey of a legendary beast? The iron grip squeezing her torso told her it was real, and she was, indeed, at the monster's mercy. The dragon's hold pinched the wooden shaft of her bow into her ribs, making Colette gasp. Gripping at its talons, she realized she was still holding the burlap sack with her dead fox inside. Then something else caught her frenzied eyes. A thick leather strap circled the beast's belly, securing what looked to be a saddle to its back.

A rider?

Could it be? The idea would have made her scoff were she not presently ensnared and being carried off to gods knew where. The calculating part of Colette's mind began to work, temporarily muting her terror. She stilled in the monster's claws and was relieved to feel its grip ease ever so slightly.

If the beast had a rider, then it had a master. If that was the case, then it was currently doing *his* bidding. What would the sort of man who could master a dragon want with *her*? Colette had a few ideas, none of them pleasant.

Straining to curl over the dragon's bulky grip, Colette grabbed at the dagger sheathed by her ankle. A half-crazed grin spread across her own lips. She may have made a mistake today...

...but she wasn't the *only* one.

2

SVEN

Finally.

Sven the Collector hunkered upon his massive saddle, basking in the thrill of having captured his bride at last. The buxom huntress had proven elusive, requiring weeks of pursuit that may have been put to better use at home, pleasing the elders. But one look at the little temptress, even from afar, had ruined him for any other woman. He wasn't sure if he should praise or curse Regna for his keen eyesight.

Now that he'd claimed her, he couldn't wait to get back to his mountain home and make her *his*. The muscles around his stomach twitched as the realities of bonding began to set in. Like all Dokiri marriages, it would be unpleasant at first. That was unavoidable, but he'd do whatever he must to ease his little bride's fears. Soon, she'd come to accept her new life, and he could turn his attention to grander things, like convincing the elders he was the right choice for their next chieftain. Sven was already well on his way toward that goal. He hoped his new bride would be a credit to him in the effort.

Regin, his mount, drew in massive wings, giving him a burst of speed and slinging them through a wispy cloud bank. The cool mist dampened Sven's dark beard, sending a chill across his flesh even through his furs. Good thing his bride had been dressed for riding. Even so, by the time they landed, she'd be glad for the dry cloak and wool dress he'd packed away. Sven craned his head over his winged *gegatu's* side, wanting to reassure himself that his catch was safe. His breath stalled in his lungs.

Angry stripes of bright red blood covered Regin's underside, the wind pulling the streaks down toward the tip of his barbed tail. His bride hung limply. The back of her dangling arm was all Sven could see.

Va kreesha!

Without thinking, Sven jammed his palms into the base of his mount's neck, urging him to dive low. Such speeds were liable to make a lowlander faint, but it couldn't be worse than whatever was causing his bride to bleed like that.

Had Regin harmed her with his talons? Unlikely. Sven had been hunting with his beast for the better part of two years, and the *gegatu* had never so much as nicked any of his prey, preferring to eat his kills alive within the heights of his icy nest. Perhaps she'd harmed herself. She'd been hunting after all. Had an arrow or an unsheathed knife found its way into her flesh even as she'd been plucked from the earth? Sven gritted his teeth and pressed harder on Regin's scales, demanding more speed.

The *gegatu* shrieked and beat his wings harder.

Below, the land was still dark with tangled trees. That foul forest had sprawled in the shadow of his people's mountain for millennia. He knew better than to descend but had little choice. Even now his bride could be dying, and he could do nothing for her from here. A narrow clearing came into focus, and Sven steered his mount with frantic purpose.

"Come on!"

A few more seconds and Sven was yanking backward on the ridges of Regin's scaly neck. The *gegatu* threw open his wings. Sven didn't wait for his mount to land. He tore off his leather gloves and began working at the bindings lashing his legs to the sides of the giant saddle. Once free, Sven heaved in anticipation, seconds scraping by like hours. Restless, he loosed his axe from its tie, ever conscious of the danger below. *Almost there.*

With the skill of a Dokiri warrior who flew far more than required, Sven gripped his axe and launched himself over Regin's body before the creature had fully touched down.

He landed hard on a slope covered in brittle black stones, his axe clattering beside him. With boots any smaller, he'd have twisted his ankle on the uneven rubble. Instead, he sprang up and darted for his mount's legs. The *gegatu* hopped and hovered on his empty foot, still clutching the unconscious woman with the other. Ducking low, Sven threw his hands up against Regin's belly.

"*Velsa lagi!*"

Responding to his master's voice, the beast opened its claws, and Sven was just able to throw an arm beneath his bride's head, catching it from impact with the rocky ground. With horror, he realized the blood *had*, indeed, come from her. It stuck to her chest and the wide sleeves of her gray riding outfit. Where was she bleeding? Golden hair with shocks of coppery red sat in a tangled mess over the limp woman's face. He batted it away, jabbing two fingers to her pale neck where a pulse should thrum.

Thump. Thump. Thump.

She was alive, and her heart was racing. His relief barely registered. Sven's brows drew as his own heart continued pounding against his ribs. He was no healer. What should he do?

Stop the bleeding, you fool.

Frowning, he dropped his gaze to the front of her jacket. Instead of a broach, it was held together by round little pieces of bronze fitted into tiny slits on the garment's opposite edge. No time to fool with that lowlander nonsense. He withdrew a knife.

The moment his blade slid out of its sheath, his bride's lashes flew open. gray-blue orbs stared up at him, and Sven froze, struck with a sense of awe that rapidly morphed into bewilderment. Fear dulling his senses, he spoke in his father's tongue.

"*Atu kaneri?*"

Her eyes narrowed but not with confusion. Sven blinked, dimly registering the malice in his bride's bright gaze. Something sliced across his flesh. He looked down. A red line swelled beneath the part of his tunic that wasn't covered by his hide jacket. Dropping his knife, his palm went automatically to his chest, covering the wound. His gaze shot to her hand, locking upon the point of the tiny dagger she'd already withdrawn into the sleeve of her coat.

The little vixen had sliced him.

He dropped her. She scrambled sideways on her hands, seeming more eager to get away from his hissing *gegatu* than from him. Sven straightened, still not fully grasping what had just happened. The woman's eyes darted between him and Regin, her movements slow and steady as if she were in the presence of some ferocious predator. Blinking, Sven scrutinized her. Was she really injured? She looked more frightened than pained. No. Not frightened. *Furious*. Then where had all that blood come from?

"Are you hurt?" he asked, this time remembering to use trade-tongue.

Rather than answer, she stood, shuffling backward so as not to turn her back on him. Instinctually, Sven lunged forward, catching her arm that shot out to strike him again. She flinched as though preparing for a blow. Crouching over her, Sven gave her a shake.

"Are. You. Hurt?"

Her face slackened in an expression of surprise that swiftly devolved into a scowl. "Worry about yourself, Barbarian."

Some of his tension left him, and he scowled right back. He'd expected his bride to show some resistance, but pulling a knife on him? As small and defenseless as she was? Was she totally mad?

The ground began to shift. A wave of vertigo crashed over him, and his vision momentarily doubled. Sven's stomach tightened and a light sweat broke out across his brow. Realization hit.

He snatched the dagger out of her hand and held it up between them. "What's on this blade?"

The little she-devil actually smirked.

Va kreesha.

Was she mad? He had to act fast. He released her, shooting to his feet. Another wave of dizziness made him stagger, and he nearly ended up on his rear as he stumbled toward Regin. Could he get them both on his mount's back in time? No. They'd need provisions. Could he, at least, remove his other weapons? His pack? The blurring at the corners of his vision told him 'no'. His tricksy bride may have just brought the mountain down on her own pretty head. The thought made him rail.

Sven swung his arms, hissing at Regin in his language. The beast turned and growled low but opened its wings to obey its master. A cyclone kicked up around Sven as the *gegatu* leapt into the air and disappeared over the trees. There was one danger to his bride eliminated.

Feet going numb, Sven dropped to his knees. He scanned the slope, searching for somewhere safe to send his bride. The sound of gravel crunching underfoot drew his gaze to the side. She was standing off at a distance, arms crossed smugly over her chest. At her devious expression, it occurred to him that he might do well to be afraid for himself.

"What did you do to me?"

She stared at him with arched brows, saying nothing. Sven fell forward on his palms, desperate to stay off the ground.

"Woman! What was on that blade?" His speech began to slur as though he'd imbibed too much wine.

Still, she refused to answer. When his elbows buckled, he rolled onto his back. That crunching sound resumed, and Sven caught sight of his bride standing over him, her eyes fixed on his. He began to pant.

"Am I going to...die?"

Her full lips pursed in a pensive look. "I'm undecided."

With that spiteful answer, everything went dark.

THE BRUTE FINALLY SUCCUMBED, his brown eyes rolling back in his head. The nightfang oil on her blade would keep him asleep for several hours. She studied him, a giant among men. Was he even human? On second thought, someone his size might only stay down for two hours. She glanced to the blood-spattered ground where the dragon had been. The barbarian might have sent it to alert other dragons with giant riders, and it might be coming back. She wouldn't be sticking around to find out.

She'd been so distracted during the flight that she wasn't even certain how far she'd been carried away from her father's land. The sun was still firmly in the east, and from it, Colette deduced that the beast had carried her south, toward the Crook-Spine Mountain range. So she turned north.

Nothing about this terrain was familiar. The trees stretched so high they completely blocked her view of the monstrous mountains that were relatively close by. Even in this clearing she couldn't find them, only knew which direction they should be. The crooked branches were barren and black, as though they'd been singed by a long-extinguished fire. And yet, she was somehow sure that those trees were still very much alive. More than that, it was as if they diffused some dark, malevolent purpose. Colette forced herself to look away. She didn't have time to contemplate the idea of sentient trees.

She made it all of three steps when a high pitched screeching rose over the nearby treeline. The sound made her jump, checking her firmly into the realm of reality. She was going to die out here unless she could come up with a plan. Traipsing blindly through the Twist, hoping to happen safely upon her father, didn't qualify. Resisting the urge to run for the nearest hiding spot, Colette assessed her options.

She needed a way out of here, and a way to protect herself as she went. Her bow lay on the ground, its string snapped. She kicked a rock across the clearing. Her quiver only held three arrows anyway. Hardly enough to be useful. All she had was her hunting knife and the tiny dagger she'd used on the barbarian. She'd pulled the sneaky blade from beneath her skirts, out of the holster she always wore about her ankle. Over the years, it had served as a deterrent to those who thought her raucous reputation translated into promiscuity. How wrong those fools had been.

As she looked around, the gravity of her situation fully sank in. She was alone without a mount, decent weapons, or provisions in one of the most dangerous places in Sestoria. Certainly the most dangerous place in her country of Morhagen.

Think, Colette. Use your head.

As her mind worked, her gaze fell unwittingly to the unconscious savage lying nearby. A man strong enough to command a dragon could be a useful asset. Of course, now that she'd poisoned him, and considering he was the one responsible for dragging her into this disaster in the first place, she should probably jot him firmly into the 'liability' category. Not to mention the issue of how she could maintain control over him.

But then, he had seemed inordinately concerned for her wellbeing, even after she'd cut him. Perhaps he could be reasoned with. She glowered in his general direction. She was grasping, but then, desperate women couldn't be choosy and, at the moment, Colette was feeling wretchedly desperate. Damn him.

She stalked over to the stranger and stared down at his sleeping face. His long brown hair was as dark as his eyes. He had it braided back and away from his bearded face, which revealed the deep cut of his high cheekbones and wide jaw. Aside from being tall, he was strong. She'd wager he was a fine cut beneath his hide and fur clothing. She'd never seen a man quite like this one. What a pity. Under different circumstances, she could imagine wanting to brush her fingers over those thick lashes instead of clawing out the eyes just beneath them. Colette frowned as something like lust tightened in her belly.

She shook her head.

If she was going to make use of this man, she'd have to keep him alive. To do that, she needed to get him somewhere safe and wait for the toxin to run its course. She glanced around until she spotted a darkened mound about halfway down the hill.

Could it be?

Perhaps fortune was tossing her a bone. After the day she'd had, she was overdue. Colette strutted around the sleeping man's body and cocked her head. Smirking, she wedged a boot against his ribs.

"Barbarian, this is going to hurt you *far* more than it hurts me."

3

SVEN

Clink. Clink. Clink.

Sven turned toward the tinny sound and groaned against the stinging in his head. His eyes scraped open over bits of dry dust. He was lying in the shadows on a cold, dirt-covered floor. The air around him was dank and musty. A cave? No. A den. Sven's arms flexed as he went to touch the low hanging ceiling above him. A tug of resistance made him pause. He reached again. His arms remained rigid against his sides.

He was bound.

Sven gasped for air and twisted against his restraints, willing his eyes to focus so that he could see what had been used to tie him. Strips of dampened cloth lashed his wrists and ankles together. His knees, too, were joined, and his elbows secured to his sides. His coat had been removed as had his fur chaps, leaving him in his hide pants and wool tunic.

Something rustled at the other side of the darkened den. An amber light glowed, illuminating a woman's wolfish gaze.

His bride.

She sat crouched against the far wall. Her elbows were slumped casually over her propped knees. A puff of vapor whirled up, obscuring her lovely features. The sweet, heavy odor of pipe smoke wafted through the air. Sven's mind reeled as the confounding woman tucked a flint and steel into the pocket of her riding coat.

A corner of her full mouth flicked upward. "Sleep well?"

Sven swallowed. *Gods, what have I gotten myself into?*

COLETTE TOOK a long drag from her pipe, relaxing at the comforting taste. The barbarian had gone still, no longer struggling against the strips of cloth she'd torn from one of her petticoats. He was staring at her, his dark eyes narrowed. She enjoyed watching his mind arrange the fragments of his memories back into place, and was especially thrilled when his face slackened with incredulity.

That's right. You're mine now, savage. How does it feel?

"Where have you taken me?" His deep voice was dry and thickly accented.

"*You* brought us to the Twist. *I* hauled your sorry ass down here for the time being. You're damn lucky there was a den at the bottom of the hill. More so that I was willing to kick you down to it. No thanks necessary."

He turned his head to the ceiling and rolled his broad shoulders in a circle. "That explains the pain."

"Oh,"—Colette flipped her freshly formed braid over her shoulder—"that's probably just the wound I gave you." After ensuring the den was empty and rolling him inside, Colette had tended to the barbarian's cut. A thread from her kerchief and a spare dress pin were handy enough. "Don't worry, I stitched it up, though I admit my needlework leaves something to be desired. I'd apologize for the scar it's going to leave but—"

Colette paused, dropping the flippant edge from her voice. "I hardly think you'll notice."

Huddled over his sleeping body, she'd barely pulled the hem of his tunic up before gasping in shock. His torso, neck to navel, was completely covered in sweeping patterns of rune-like scars. Her mouth had dropped at the exotic sight; it was at once alarming and mesmerizing.

The barbarian surprised her with an impish grin across his bearded face. "Stripped me down, did you?"

"I've seen more of you than I would have liked, yes."

That was a lie. Colette had seen precisely as much as she wanted, which was to say she'd seen all of him, brazenly following the path of his scars across his arms and legs as well as shamelessly satisfying years of maidenly curiosity. She couldn't have asked for a finer study. No regrets.

"Shame I was asleep."

Colette ignored the urge to crack a smile. She had to admit, she'd expected a touch more fear from this man. He was impressively confident for a prisoner, particularly one whose jailer was a young woman. He could probably stand to be brought down a peg. Or three. She blew a puff of smoke in his direction. "I liked you better that way."

"Sharp tongue. Sharp claws. Is there any part of you that's soft?"

Colette raised an imperious brow. "You'll never find out, savage."

"My name is Sven the Collector."

"Collector of what? Women minding their own business?"

He grinned, flashing straight white teeth. "Among other things."

Snide bastard. "What did you mean to do with me?"

"Untie me, and I'll tell you."

"Are women that stupid where you come from?"

He cocked his head, an odd-looking gesture while lying in the dirt. "What are you worried about? That I'll punish you for defending yourself?"

"More like you'll try to abduct me again."

His tone took on a serious edge. "So why didn't you run?"

Leaning forward, she smirked. "Because you're going to get me out of these woods."

"Gladly." He wiggled around, glancing pointedly down at his bindings and back up at her.

Her lips thinned. "Let's make a few things understood between us. First, you're not going to call your beast back."

His dark brows drew together. "Strange. I could have sworn to the Sky Father that you just asked me to get you out of these woods."

"I did, and you are. On foot."

He regarded her for a long moment, his mouth a hard line. "You want to hike through the Twist?"

She stared him down, unflinching.

The barbarian scoffed. "Are you insane?"

The words had barely left his mouth when she lunged for him. Startled, he tried to rise, but she swung a leg over his chest, knocking him back down. His entire body was taut as he struggled to right himself, but Colette's weight and her deft knots were enough to keep him supine.

She unsheathed the same dagger she'd used to cut him before and shoved the tip just beneath his bearded chin. "You tell me."

He arched his neck, trying to get away from the steel point. "Gods, I've got good taste!"

Colette watched his nervous smile with silent fascination. All things considered, he was remarkably calm, but he couldn't hide his speeding heartbeat. She felt it thrumming through his chest beneath her skirts. Her lips peeled back in triumph.

"Swear an oath to your gods, to your 'Sky Father', that you won't call your beast down."

Though he glared at her, his dark eyes flickered with uncertainty. "You're going to be the death of me, Woman."

He wasn't taking her seriously. Colette could remedy that. She moved the knife up and pressed the tip into the swell of his bottom lip. With her free hand, she scooped up a nearby stone and shoved it against the closed corner of his mouth.

"You'll swear to me, or I swear to *you* that I'll open your mouth and use my knife to make sure you can't call anyone ever again."

Sven met her gaze. Colette sat still as a stone, refusing to back down from the challenge.

He spoke, careless of the knife piercing his skin. "As mad as you are beautiful."

That caught her off guard. He thought her beautiful? In and of itself, it wasn't especially shocking. She'd been called beautiful countless times, and not only by her father. But, like this? With blood dried into her clothes, and her knife held against his flesh? She supposed she might be beautiful in the same way a she-wolf looked beautiful tearing into a stag. How strangely suitable... A sneaky flash of delight made her belly tighten. She reminded herself not to blink.

His breath was strained and thready despite all other appearances of ease. "Just to be clear, you trust me not to call my *gegatu* but not enough to let me fly you out of this death trap?"

Was he the type of man who kept his word? She could only hope. In the meantime, she'd prepare for his betrayal. Better to manage it here than in the sky. Whatever else happened, she couldn't allow that beast of his back into play.

"Trust has nothing to do with it. If you break your vow and call your mount, I'll have time to sink my blade into your gut.

But if I let you call your mount and *then* you decide to betray me..." She cocked her head. "What's my recourse?"

"Would it appease you if I let you hold your little dagger to my belly as we flew?"

Her eyes sparked. "*No* dragons."

"Wyverns."

"What?"

"My mount is a wyvern. Not a dragon."

She frowned, irritated she had no witty response to that. Why was he so calm? So smug? She ground the point of her blade down until a single prick of blood swelled onto his lip. It wouldn't be enough to poison him again. Probably.

He groaned, and Colette felt the vibration in his chest rise up along her inner thighs. Somewhere low in her belly, the strangest sensation came to life, warm and pleasing. Startled, she pressed harder on the knife.

"I'm about three seconds from slicing out your tongue, Savage."

"Oh, I think you'd regret that in the long term."

When she started to wedge the rock against his teeth, the savage thrust his head away into the dirt.

"Okay. Okay. I swear to Regna I won't call my mount."

"Swear you'll bring me safely through the Twist or die trying."

Nodding, he shrugged. "Probably just die, though."

"Swear it!"

"I swear it. Now kindly get your knife out of my face." He glanced down at her legs. "You can keep your thighs wrapped around me if you want."

Colette huffed and climbed off. The initial thrill of victory dissipated like a morning mist. Silence stretched between them as she wrestled with what needed to come next. Spine straightening, she began to untie his bindings. His eyes bore into her, making her doubt her actions. There was nothing for it. He was no good to her trussed up like a pheasant. He remained perfectly still as she loosened the last of the ties.

Meeting his gaze, Colette eased away from him. She wouldn't have him thinking she was afraid.

Rubbing his unbound wrists, Sven sat up. Even on the ground, his head almost brushed against the dirt ceiling of the tiny den. The man was easily three times her weight, though there seemed to be no spare flesh around his well-toned muscles. Colette was grateful she'd had enough cloth to tie him in the first place. She'd have been no match against him otherwise.

"What's your name?" he asked, the timbre of his voice light.

"Colette."

Releasing his wrists, he nodded thoughtfully. He gave her a long, lingering look from head to toe. Her skin prickled, and she inclined her chin.

"Give me your knife, Colette."

She scoffed. "Why would I do that?"

"Because I'm going to take it from you if you don't. But don't worry, you'll get it back."

"Oh? In my heart, perhaps?"

His lips curled. "I wouldn't ruin your pretty breasts."

The arrogance! Who did this man think he was? And why in the hells was she cracking a smile? With effort, Colette turned it into a sneer. "What do you want with it?"

Without warning, the barbarian shot forward on his knees. Colette jerked back even as she took a swing at him with her dagger. He caught her wrist in an iron grip that seemed to span half her forearm. It was obvious he'd been prepared for that move, especially when his next sent the air rushing out of her lungs. She gasped, too stunned to fight back until he'd already settled the length of his body snugly against hers, as well as pinned her wrists over her head with a single hand. He used the other to pluck the dagger from her clenched fist.

A shudder wracked through Colette's limbs. She was at this hulking man's mercy. She didn't dare struggle. She wouldn't give him the satisfaction. Instead, she gritted her teeth. "How dare you?"

He pressed his chest into hers. "Easily. Now, let's make a few *more* things understood between us. When we find water to clean this little blade with, it's all yours. In the meantime, I think I'll hold on to it."

Colette's mind fired, trying to think about what she could do. All thoughts came to a screeching halt as Sven's free hand reached down and grasped at her skirt. Slowly, deliberately, he began to draw it upward. Colette gasped, and her whole body jerked when she felt his fingertips grazing her bare calf. To her horror, a whimper of fear rose in her throat.

His eyes locked on hers, and Colette held her breath.

Suddenly, he was off her. A current of cool air hit, replacing the warmth of his chest. She shot up. What had just happened? Why was he stopping? And, by the gods, why did she feel *excited*? Without thinking, her hands flew to her leg, covering the place where he'd touched her. The flesh there burned as if branded. It was a sweet, lingering heat.

Sitting on his knees, Sven raised a hand. In it, he held her longer hunting knife. She'd exchanged its place with her poisoned dagger, hoping to keep its existence a secret. He flipped it smoothly around so that the handle was extended in her direction. "You can keep this one."

"How did you..."

He grinned, capturing every bit of the smugness she'd cast at him earlier. Damn, it looked good on him. She cursed the rising flush of her cheeks.

"You've got courage, woman. I'll give you that. And no small amount of wit. But you're not a fighter. Unless you obey me, you're probably going to die out here and so will I, trying to keep your willful ass safe. I have a hundred better things to do than wandering through a deadly wilderness but, that's the position you've put us in. So we're going to do things *my* way. Do you understand?"

The nerve of this savage. No one, not even her father, had ever spoken to her this way. A baffling sense of division tore her senses in two—fascination and utter fury.

She leaned forward. "You have no right!"

"Oh, little she-devil, I'm *Na Dokiri*. I have *every* right."

4

COLETTE

A narrow path of afternoon sunlight lit the bottom of the rocky ravine. All around it, gray shadows seemed to drench the area in oppressive doubt. Even the air smelled cold. Barren. Colette turned to Sven, ignoring her unease. He'd started up the slope.

"Where are you going?"

"Stay here," he ordered over his shoulder.

Huffing, Colette followed. Ahead of her, Sven glanced toward the sky and shook his head, though he said nothing. The glint of light reflected on steel lying at the top of the hill. There, on the ground, was a large double-bitted axe she hadn't noticed before. Sven went directly to it and snapped it up, inspecting it for damage.

"Where's your bow?"

Colette nodded at the ground where her useless bow lay. The broken string was still tied to either nock. Sven stuffed a hand into his coat and withdrew a fresh cord in the same way her brother Gareth would withdraw sweets from his pocket. Like Gareth, as soon as she grabbed for it, he snatched it up and away from her.

She glared at him.

"You only have three arrows. Try to conserve them," he said.

"Thank the gods I have you here to advise me."

He tossed the string at her.

Colette caught it easily and immediately set to restringing her bow.

"We'll head north and make our way downhill until we find water. A stream should lead us to the forest's edge."

She frowned. "The river lets out of the Twist thirty miles west from my father's lands. We should just focus on going north."

"We won't save any time if we get lost in the forest, and neither of us knows this terrain. We'll follow the water."

"And if it dead-ends us into a lake?"

Sven shrugged and swung his axe around as if testing the balance. "I didn't see any lakes from the sky. But, if it does, then it's back to your plan."

His axe was adorned with rings of claws and teeth from at least a dozen different creatures, none of them natural. The end of his braid, too, was secured by the vertebrae of some fallen creature that she didn't recognize. Charming.

Colette leaned away, her gaze flickering to him. "Why are you called 'The Collector'?"

They started back down the hill. "My father named me after I completed the *veligneshi*."

"What's that?"

"A rite of passage. The men of my clan must kill a fiend from beneath our mountain to be considered *Na Dokiri*. Most riders kill one. I brought back the heads of a dozen."

"Are you a show-off, then? Or do you have something to prove?"

Without slowing, he spat on the ground. "Yes."

What to make of this man? She licked her lips. "Why do your people bother with the killing?"

"To protect all the lands below us from the evil that resides in our mountain."

They reached the bottom of the hill.

"Lands like mine?"

He nodded.

"How charitable of you."

Sven's face was turned away from her, his eyes peering into the shadow of the dense treeline. His expression was tight and calculating as he took the first step into the darkness. He held an assisting hand back to her. "It's not charity."

Ignoring his hand, Colette followed him into the forest, then immediately wished she'd accepted his offer, if only to feel the presence of another living being. The forest was cold and still, the screeching of predatory birds the only sign of life. The stink of mold and carrion wormed through the thickness of the air, invading her nostrils. Colette shifted when something scratched at her legs. Already, the layers of her skirts had been invaded by blood-hungry brambles. *Swiving hells.* Even the leaf-bare trees seemed sinister. Their gnarled branches choked the sun from the sky, plunging the land into eternal twilight.

A fine place for a grave.

Swallowing, she glanced at Sven.

Or two.

On an inhale, Colette thrust back her shoulders and started down the now gentle slope of the dirt-packed ground. "Oh? And what do your people get out of protecting foreign strangers?"

Sven's footsteps kept pace behind her. "Those who succeed are given a name, *and* the right to claim a bride."

"The women of your clan must be thrilled."

"Not usually at first."

"What? With such considerate, hospitable men like yourself to tend to them?"

"You wouldn't mind my hospitality. My tending even less so."

She choked on a short-lived laugh. Awareness made her lower her voice. "Was *that* your grand scheme? Make me your bride?"

"I didn't know you'd be such a thorn in my ass."

Colette clenched her fists. "Well, let me relieve you. I'm to be married to someone else."

Just as he was stepping over a fallen branch, Sven hesitated before resuming an even stride. "That poor man."

"On the contrary, he finds me utterly alluring."

"Then I'm sure his eyes are intact. But, tell me, is he hard of hearing?"

Colette's mouth flattened into a tight smile. "In fact, he possesses all his faculties. Why, he can even find *willing* women to wed him."

"He sounds like a prize. I'm sorry to deprive you of him."

Better here than there.

Had she really just thought that? Colette frowned. She was currently roaming through the Twist with only a savage who had kidnapped her for company. And yet, she felt oddly exhilarated, even more so as she verbally sparred with the cocky male who, if she was honest with herself, was delicious to look at, scars and all. Perhaps she should remind them both of their tenuous relationship.

"Yes, he will be worried about me but get me out of this forest, savage, and I might ask my father not to take your head."

"How generous." The bastard actually smiled. "I'm dying to know, are all women where you come from as bloodthirsty as you?"

"Only ones who can put a barbarian on his back."

"Oh, little hellion, anytime you want me on my back, you just say the word."

That was it. She was done talking to him. The barbarian had an answer for everything and, damn him, for the time being, she'd run out of retorts. How unlike her. It had to be this godsforsaken place. The atmosphere was getting to her. She'd wait a while until she'd adjusted, then she'd rally.

You win this round, barbarian. Enjoy it while it lasts.

For the next few hours, Colette took it upon herself to make life as inconvenient for him as possible. If he walked left, she veered right. If he stopped to inspect something, which he often did, she continued on. Once he caught up, she'd take great pleasure in drawing shrub branches forward as she passed and allowing them to whip backward, occasionally catching him in the face. At one point, she realized the way she sneezed irritated him, so she was sure to develop a sudden rash of hay fever. Colette observed the tense set of his shoulders with gleeful satisfaction. How much longer before he snapped?

Eventually, the sound of water drew both their attention until they were walking faster and faster, their thirst driving them on. Colette froze when she saw the creek ahead. The steep embankment cut a good ten feet downward, barely leaving a place to safely stand or collect a drink. Oblivious to her hesitation, Sven drew forward and wasted no time hopping down, his big hand gripping a nearby branch for support.

Colette crept up to the edge and, leaning back, peered down. Her companion was crouched low, scooping up water and bringing it to his face.

She bit her lip. "Are you sure it's safe to drink?"

After a long swallow, Sven answered, panting, "It's not like we have an alternative."

Arms crossed over her chest, she nodded once. A few more drinks and Sven held a hand up to her. A sudden, terror-filled image flashed across her mind, and she took a hasty step away. "Don't pull me in."

Sven stilled, his brow furrowing. Then a devious smile played at his lips. "Why? Do you think you deserve it? Can't say I disagree."

"Just...don't."

Something in her voice must have caught his attention because his smug demeanor melted away. Sober faced, he nodded and reached back up to her.

After a breath, Colette accepted his help, though the muscles in her body were painfully rigid. Huddling against the creekbank wall, she clung to Sven's ankle with one hand and drank with the other. Was her fear obvious? Or was he a typical, inattentive male? Gods, she hoped so. When she finished drinking, her ears were thoroughly red. She couldn't climb back up the bank fast enough, and as soon as she crested the top, she skittered several yards away.

As she walked, the sudden buzz of coin-sized flies had her swatting at the air. One flew directly at the side of her head, its drone drowning out the sound of her own startled yip. Flailing her arms, she began running, but the insects only seemed to grow more numerous until the air in front of her was a thick, swarming curtain. She started to scream, but choked when she felt the brush of opaque wings against her lips.

An arm swooped around her waist and hauled her to the side. Knowing it was Sven, she hurried in the direction he pulled until the din of the flies died down to a distant hum.

"Swiving hell!"

"For Regna's sake, keep your voice down, woman."

"I hate this place!" she gritted, obeying, despite herself.

He shoved something into her palm. "Stay here."

Looking down, she saw that he'd returned her dagger to her, the wooden handle damp with creek water. She hadn't actually expected him to return it to her. Swallowing, her gaze flicked up.

"Where are you going?" She took a step after him until it became clear he was headed straight back into the filthy swarm. "Sven, what are you doing?"

"They gather at something's corpse. I'm going to look at it."

"But of course. Why not?"

Ignoring her, he continued on, until his figure dissolved into the screen of flying vermin. Still uneasy, Colette hissed after him. "Great. Just wonderful. Maybe you'll find a pretty new tooth for your collection. Why, you could even stir things up a bit and take its balls. They seem more your fashion anyway. They'd go nicely tied around your neck. You'd like that, wouldn't you?"

Silence.

Pacing, Colette clutched at the bowstring slung across her chest. "Sven! I am *not* coming in there after you!"

When he finally emerged, the paleness of his face quickly robbed her of any relief. Arms extended, she took a step toward him. "What is it?"

"It's a bear. It's been slaughtered..." he seemed to weigh his words, "...messily."

Colette's skin chilled. "What killed it?"

"I have a few ideas. We need to keep moving. The smell will draw scavengers."

Chastened, Colette nodded and walked with him along the creek bank, though she was careful to keep Sven between it and herself. The shadows grew deeper as they went along, the strangled daylight succumbing to the grip of dusk.

With heightened senses, Colette began to pay attention to the kind of things that drew Sven's attention and caused him to linger from time to time. Tree-bark scratches several inches thick, muddy tracks the size of cartwheels. Each sign heightened her own wariness and soon it was all she could do to follow Sven and keep an eye open for small game she might hunt.

By the time they stopped, they'd found nothing to eat, but then, nothing had found them either. Colette decided she couldn't complain. Not about food, at least. What disturbed her more was their total lack of shelter.

Sven dropped his axe and sat against the trunk of a cabin-thick tree. "We'll sleep in shifts to make sure nothing can sneak up on us."

"Shouldn't we start a fire?"

"No. Not unless you're certain there's nothing in here that's attracted to light."

Did that mean they'd have eaten her kill raw? Colette was almost grateful she'd seen no prey. Walking several feet away, she leaned her bow against the tree.

Sven patted the ground next to where he sat with knees propped up. "Come sleep here. I'll take first watch since I already had such a refreshing nap today."

Colette eyed the spot next to him. She'd never slept so close to anyone before, much less a grown man. She thought of the claw marks in the trees and took her seat. The moment her bottom touched the ground, bone-deep weariness overwhelmed her. This had been the most harrowing day of her life and now she had a feeling she was about to experience her most terrifying night. She sank down to the cold dirt and presented the savage with her back. With her elbow tucked beneath her head, Colette welcomed sleep.

It didn't come.

Lying still, the noises of the forest around them were suddenly amplified tenfold. Had she thought this place quiet? Something hissed and splashed into the bubbling creek nearby. A falling branch clattered to the ground. Overhead, the leather wings of bats rustled. Though they were long gone, Colette could still hear that horrid buzzing of flies in her ear. The high-pitched wailing of some distant creature finally made her eyes pop open. She twisted to glance back at Sven.

"If you touch me tonight, I'll put my dagger in your eye."

He was sitting casually against the trunk, axe slung across his lap. "Can you do me a favor and make it my ear?"

Colette huffed. "You've been warned, savage."

"That I have. Now go to sleep. We need to get started as early as possible tomorrow."

Something was breathing. Or was it a whisper? Whatever it was, it was deep and heavy, seeming to fill the entire forest. She squeezed her eyes shut, willing herself to ignore it.

Eventually, she spoke, trying her best to sound annoyed. "What's making that sound?"

"Which one?"

"The—" She searched for the right word. "Moaning one."

"It's the wind."

"There isn't any wind in here."

"Above the canopy. It catches the branches and bends the wood. It pulls a moan deep down to their roots."

Colette's shoulders relaxed the barest of inches. Then she frowned and turned over so she was facing him. "Isn't it driving you crazy?"

He kept his eyes on the woods. "No. It sounds like home."

"I thought you said you live in the mountains."

"I do. We sleep in caves. Underground, there's an ever-present hum. We call it Helig's Song."

He had a pleasant voice. So long as he was talking, Colette could ignore the lurid orchestra all around her. "What's living in a cave like?"

"I'll tell you tomorrow."

She fiddled with the sleeve of her coat and fought the

impulse to squirm. "I'm sure savages can get used to anything. Maybe if I were wild like you, I could just ignore it."

"Stop talking, Colette. I know it's hard for you, but you'll fall asleep faster."

Thwarted, she turned back over and tried to focus on the sound of her own breathing. The better part of an hour stretched by, and though she was exhausted, she was no closer to sleep than she'd been at the start. On top of it all, she was getting cold. How she longed for her featherdown bed and the security of her chamber's four stone walls. Swiving hells, right now she could even be grateful as a guest in Lord Myron's household. At least the chattering of her teeth was mildly distracting.

Something settled over her back, and Colette jumped, only to relax when she realized it was Sven's forearm. He was using her like an armrest, and his heat covered most of the length of her body. Was he keeping her warm on purpose? Or simply making himself comfortable?

His low voice cut into her thoughts. "The men you ride with, who are they?"

"My father, and my *five* older brothers."

He didn't seem the least bit fazed by her proclamation, which was mildly irritating. Most people showed a modicum of wariness that she had so many, presumably, loving male protectors at her disposal. As well they should.

"How come you're the only woman who ever goes on the hunts?"

Colette paused, her mind working. "You've been watching me? For how long?"

She could almost hear the shrug in his voice. "A few weeks."

No shame. "And you chose now to abduct me because?"

"You were alone."

"Strange. I wouldn't have figured a man who can bend a wyvern to his will to be so cautious."

"And I wouldn't have figured a woman clever enough to set a trap in the sky foolish enough to ride into the Twist alone."

There was no reproach in his words. In fact, Colette had the vaguest sense that he found one action as intriguing as the other. Pride warmed her from the inside out, and her lips curved into a soft smile.

She was beginning to drowse when something occurred to her. He wasn't urging her to be silent. In fact, he'd started this conversation so nonchalantly, it was obvious he'd known she was lying awake. Was he trying to put her at ease? She considered the intentional nuisance she'd spent the day making of herself and felt a twinge of guilt. Maybe tomorrow she wouldn't snap branches in his face?

Before she could talk herself out of it, Colette leaned back so that she was tucked closer into his warm side. She sighed. That was better. So long as he was obliging, she'd continue to pelt him with questions until she managed to drift off.

"How did you tame your mount?"

"Nerve and a lot of patience."

She yawned. "Do all the men where you come from have winged steeds?"

"Those who don't die, yes. It's our first rite of passage, the one that marks us as men."

Incredible. Colette didn't try to hide the awe in her voice. "How many rites are there?"

"Only one more."

"What's that?" Her eyelids began to droop. "Castrate a demigod?"

Sven chuckled. "Something far more perilous." He flexed his fingers across her hip. As Colette faded off, she thought she heard him mumble. "Regna help me."

5

COLETTE

A haunting shriek, unlike anything Colette had ever heard, echoed through the early-dawn forest. Beside her, Sven woke with a jolt and was on his feet in a shadowy flash.

Colette's throat went dry as parchment. "What is that?"

The stillness of Sven's body as he listened made Colette's panic rise. She went still, too, turning her ear toward the haunting sound. She'd been terrified most of the night, the barbarian's strangely comforting presence the only thing that kept her from running hysterically through the woods. Despite her fear, her watch had been uneventful, and Colette eventually relaxed, resting a hand over Sven's shoulder just to assure herself she wasn't alone. Now her savage was tense as a bowstring and that didn't bode well for either of them.

Colette glanced up at the canopy, searching for the morning sun. Her stomach leapt into her throat. The trees had moved overnight. She was sure of it. This was not the same forest she'd fallen asleep in. Did Sven notice it, too? She turned to ask when the howling noise rose up again, making the hairs of her arms stand on end. Her jaw snapped shut. They had bigger concerns.

"Get up. We have to go." Sven reached down and plucked her up by the arm, his face still turned toward the trees. In the subdued light, Colette could just make out the deepening lines of his face.

"The creature, it can't be too close, right?" Colette didn't even know what 'it' was, but she needed Sven to agree with her. The sound had come from miles away. Surely, they were safe from it. Surely.

"Anywhere is too close."

Not much had seemed to shake this man before. What could have him so anxious now? She didn't want to find out. Colette turned west and started to hurry when Sven's hand clamped firmly around her wrist. She turned just in time to see him set his eyes on the thick canopy above and let out a series of rapid whistles so loud she wanted to cover her ears. Her brows drew together.

"What are you doing?"

He answered without looking at her. "Calling my mount."

Colette's stomach seized, and she tore her wrist from his hand. "What?"

He whistled again, and Colette's hand went to her knife. Her mind raced. Should she stop him? Urge him on? She didn't know. Colette wasn't usually an indecisive person, but then, she'd never been in such a terrible situation. What exactly were her options?

Sven whistled again, the gnarled branches of the trees seeming to absorb the noise. He muttered something in his language that must have been a curse then grabbed at her wrist again.

"We need to move." He tugged on her, making her stumble through the brambles and across filthy quagmires.

"What's going on?" she demanded, hoping the anger in her voice concealed her utter panic.

"We're being hunted."

"That creature must have been miles away."

"It's a brujit. It will catch up to us."

A brujit? Vague snippets of memory crested the surface of her mind. The brujit were said to be men who'd fed on their own kind until madness took them and evil twisted their bodies. Though they ate anything they could find, their hunger was supposedly insatiable and the flesh of men their deepest craving. Colette's brother, Willam, said that one had been defeated outside the village of Windslope. They'd cut open its belly only to find the decomposing body of a young child, swallowed whole.

Her mouth fell open. "How do you know?"

"I've seen one before. Its stride was longer than you are tall, and it's smart enough to track us."

"What makes you so sure it will?"

"Because we're its favored prey."

So the stories must be true. She picked up her pace. Sven continued to whistle, the tension in his shoulders building with every unanswered call. Finally, he tossed her hand away.

"Damn you, woman. Thanks to you and that asinine oath, my mount's gone too far away to hear us."

Colette's lips thinned, but she kept moving. "It's not as if you hold your oaths sacred. Obviously."

"Do you want to be eaten?" He didn't wait for an answer. "Neither do I. But that's what's going to happen if we don't find a way out of this damn forest soon."

Eaten. He said it so matter-of-factly. Colette's blood turned cold at the image. She didn't acknowledge his words. Couldn't.

"And if your mount had shown up? What would you have done then, hmm?"

"I would have taken us back to my home in Bedmeg."

She scoffed, putting on a burst of speed so she could throw a scowl at him over her shoulder. "Oh, so you wouldn't even have tried to honor your oath? Not even the spirit of it?"

He glared back at her, and she could see his fist clenching around the handle of his macabre axe. Was she getting to him?

"I don't know why I'm even the slightest bit surprised. You kidnapped me once already. Apparently, honor isn't high on your list of priorities."

"It's my right to claim you, and I don't have time to go looking for another bride."

Heat rose up in Colette's face as well as something else. Hurt. *That* was his opinion of her? Was she interchangeable with any other woman? Yesterday, she could have sworn she'd made an impression on him. Hadn't she earned a modicum of his respect? Not that it should matter. But, by the gods, it had pleased her to think that a man, especially one as handsome as Sven, might be impressed, even attracted to her wildness. How refreshing and...intriguing. Now that satisfaction wilted like a blossom held up to the flame.

She swallowed hard and gritted her teeth. "And here I thought I'd been making it clear as glass that I'm more trouble than I'm worth."

"You're troublesome, alright. But I've invested too much time in you at this point. You'll suit my purposes well enough."

Humiliation welled in a knot at her throat. Had she really been charmed by this heathen just last night? Maybe mother was right. Perhaps she did lack judgment. "Oh, savage, if you think I've been difficult thus far, you haven't seen anything yet! I swear I'll make you regret the day you ever laid eyes on me."

"Too late." He nudged her forward. "Hurry up."

She wanted to dig her heels in the ground just to gainsay him, but she remembered that otherworldly howling and kept moving. There would be time to make him suffer, after they were out of danger. And she *would* make him suffer.

Some of the pressure in Sven's chest eased as the cobalt light filtering through the trees brightened to a dull gray. He was unusually irritable and unsure why. Probably because he was being hunted like a rabbit with this spitfire of a woman in tow. What had started as a dangerous trek had morphed into an all-out race for survival. What had he been thinking, agreeing not to call his mount?

You weren't thinking. Not with your head, at least.

It was true. Sure, the little firebrand had forced an oath on him, but he had no great qualms in breaking such a pointless promise. After all, it wasn't as if he'd planned to set her free once they'd escaped the forest. So what had been the point of all this? Hiking on, he rolled his eyes at himself.

He'd wanted to impress her. And what man wouldn't? He'd been tricked and effectively dominated by a tiny temptress who'd had the nerve to make demands of him. Of *him*. Sven had never met anyone like her and was certain he never would again.

Shame and irritation had nettled him since the moment he'd woken in her clutches. What must she think of him? She'd had so little trouble managing what was supposed to be her own claiming. Yesterday, it had seemed worth the risk to show her exactly what he was capable of and, if he was being honest, to reclaim some of his injured pride. But now? His foolishness might have cost them their very lives. Utterly idiotic.

Now that he could see clearly through the shadows, Sven began to slow, diverting his path toward the sound of the nearby stream. He peered over the edge of the embankment at the moving water. The surface reflected the minimal light with an inky sheen that marbled as it ran. The bed was perhaps twenty feet across. Hopefully not too deep. He tossed down his axe and began to undo the fastenings of his coat.

Colette came up behind him, her arms bound across her chest. "What are you doing?"

"Take off your clothes."

"Excuse me?"

Sven inhaled sharply, trying to ignore the obstinate clip in her tone. "Or don't. I don't care."

Not entirely honest.

"But we're going to be walking through the stream, so it'd be better if you did. Else you'll be sleeping in a wet coat tonight. Assuming we survive that long."

"I'm not getting in the water."

Sven paused, jaw clicking. "The brujit is intelligent. It will follow our tracks. The water will hide them. Our scent, too. We'll walk a few hours then get out when we find a rock bank."

"I can't swim."

"You shouldn't have to."

"Go splash about if it pleases you. I'll walk along the edge."

Sven was fast losing hold on what little patience he had left. He turned fully toward her, his stance wide. "Take off your coat, Colette."

She looked him in the eye. "No."

"We don't have time for your antics."

"And I didn't have time to be kidnapped. But here I am."

His voice dropped low in warning, "Don't test me, woman."

She jutted her chin.

The little vixen was asking for it, and right then, he was all too willing to give it to her. "Fine."

Sven lunged for her, and she threw herself backward, trying to escape his outstretched arms. As they fell, Sven caught her by the hem of her riding dress. He could hear the air leaving her lungs as she collided with the ground. Clamping his fist around her ankle, he dragged her forward across the dirt-packed ground. He looked up just in time to see the bottom of her other boot careening into his face.

"*Va kreesha!*" Sven released her, his hands flying to cover his broken nose. He roared as the little shrew turned over and scrambled away. A rush of fury made him forget his blood-smattered face. He lifted himself to his hands and knees and launched himself forward, just missing her.

Now she was on her feet and running like the mountain wind. She would regret that.

He was up in a second and closing in on her after a few more. Sven could tell she knew what was about to happen. Her hand went to her knife belt. He charged, catching that hand in one of his own and using his other arm to snatch her about the waist. Spinning them both, he caught the impact of their fall. The knife went flying out of her fist. Colette screamed, and Sven loosened his grip, only for her to flip in his arms and start scratching at him like the hell-cat she was.

"Colette, stop!"

She didn't.

He tried to grab her wrists, but she was swinging them madly. Right about the time he caught a fist in the throat, Sven decided to roll her. He took an inordinate amount of satisfaction in hearing her grunt as his weight settled over her. It was short-lived. She threw a knee into his groin.

Sven groaned, his entire body seizing in pain.

Colette threw herself to the side, trying to scoot out from beneath him. Pointless. He weighed too much. She screamed her frustration, and Sven clapped a palm over her mouth.

"Quiet! Are you insane?"

She bit him.

Damn her. Enough was enough. Keeping a hold on her, he climbed to his feet and snapped her over his shoulder. Her red-blonde hair went flying as she folded against his body and immediately began thrashing. Somehow, he managed to belt his axe with one hand while keeping ahold of his bride with the other.

"Put me down! Put me down, you—"

Sven didn't recognize the next several words that came pouring from her pretty little mouth, but he comprehended their meaning just fine. She started to yank on his hair. With his free hand, he gave her rump a slap and grinned wickedly at her shriek of rage. He started off toward the creek. Hiking through the forest in wet clothes wasn't ideal, but knowing the little she-demon on his back would be suffering the same made his fate acceptable.

As Sven climbed down the slope, Colette fought him like a woman possessed. He ignored her. The chill of the water was far too icy for summer. When her feet touched the surface, he nearly lost his grip.

"Sven! Stop!" She twisted and struck. She was aiming for his groin again.

"Damn it, woman! Must everything be war with you?"

Sven leapt into the center of the creek, knowing the chest-deep water would rob her momentum for such a vicious attack. Colette gasped, her entire body going still. Stunned by the cold, no doubt. At least her legs were all that was in it. Sven huffed in victory and started walking with the current.

Out of nowhere, Colette began weeping. Her whole body shook with it. "Sven, please! Stop. Take me back!"

Her hands, which had been slapping and scratching at him only moments before, were now gripping his shoulders with white-knuckled intensity. Her arms went straight, elbows locking as she pressed herself away from his back. She turned her tear-streaked face up to the stunted canopy, away from the water's dark surface.

Sven's stride slowed. What was this? Another trick? Did the woman have no shame? His aching balls reminded him she did not. He gave her a shake.

"Quiet! You're going to draw every damn creature in this forest."

"Sven." She choked on a sob. "I'm begging you, *please* take me back! I'll do anything you ask. *Anything*."

He frowned. That didn't sound right. Suddenly, he remembered the odd look she had yesterday when she'd been about to get a drink and told him not to pull her in. Something in her eyes had struck him as more than mild concern that he'd try to get revenge on her for childish shenanigans. She'd said she couldn't swim. Was she afraid of water?

He tugged on her thighs, pulling her waist down into the current, so he could better see her face. She shoved her fingers into his scalp and squeezed his head to her chest, effectively smothering him with her breasts. He strained for air as she snaked her legs around his body, crushing his ribs. He struggled to get his hands between their bodies.

"Colette, relax!"

She didn't. In fact, she somehow tensed further. Her limbs shook, though he couldn't tell if it was from strain or fear. Her body heaved on gaping pants as though she expected to lose the power of breath at any moment. He stopped trying to peel her away.

"Easy, woman. Easy."

Her cries picked up again. "Please, Sven. *Please*."

The woman was terrorized. No wonder she'd fought him. He'd thought she was simply being contrary. He swallowed the guilt stinging the back of his throat. If he'd known, he would have gone about this differently. Should he take her back to the bank?

He started to turn then stopped himself. Nothing had

changed. They were still being hunted, and they were still in mortal danger. He had to get her to safety. For now, that meant sticking to his plan. But how was he going to get her through this?

Sven slid his arms around her back and tucked her more securely over his hips. The movement drew her closer to the waterline and a strangled moan rose up out of her throat.

He murmured into her ear, "Shh. It's all right. You're safe."

She whimpered and continued attempting to scurry up his body. Sven held her in place with a lock-arm grip, careful not to hurt her. He was going to be carrying her for a while, and he needed her low in the water where he wouldn't fatigue and, more importantly, where he could watch where he was going.

"I can't swim," she cried, the hitch in her voice making her sound far younger than she was.

"I've got you."

"Please take me back. Please."

"I will, *mu hamma*. As soon as we're safe, I will."

She buried her face into his neck. Sven could feel the heat of her tears on his skin. He started to stroke at her water-corded hair but stopped when she gave another whimper. From that point on, he kept his hands planted firmly around her body and stuck to nuzzling her with the bearded side of his face. They waded on through the water and all the while he whispered soft encouragements against the shell of her ear.

At some point, he remembered that she'd broken his nose and that even now he might still have blood on his chin. Shouldn't he be a little angry? He wasn't. He was aroused. That was hardly surprising considering the most beautiful woman he'd ever seen had her legs wrapped tightly around his waist. But it was more than that. Colette holding on to him like this, as if he were all that was keeping her well and sane, was oddly satisfying.

Eventually, her breathing began to even out. The water was cold, but the warmth shared between them kept things bearable. Colette relaxed in his arms, her temple sagging against his shoulder.

"That's it. I have you. Try to rest."

She sighed. "You're such a bastard."

There was no sting in her words, and Sven had to smile. "I'm still not putting you down."

She scoffed but said nothing.

The better part of another hour went by and, finally, she succumbed to sleep. Her slender muscles eased around him. The half-night's rest had done little for her, and fighting him had surely sapped what energy she'd gained. It was just as well. He'd carry her like this for hours, and not only because he had to.

Suddenly, he realized exactly what had been eating at him. It wasn't that Colette was unsuitable for him, it was because he'd been unconvinced he was suitable for *her*. Did a woman like her need anyone? Need *him*?

Apparently, she did. At least, sometimes.

Excitement fluttered in his stomach, and he tightened his hold on her.

That's enough for me.

6

COLETTE

Colette watched as Sven tossed a few more sticks onto the tiny fire they'd built. The heat of the flames licked at her damp under-shift, raising goosebumps on her legs. The serendipitous cave they'd found was narrow but deep enough they didn't fear drawing predators with the flicker of the light.

Most of their clothes lay out on the ground as close to the fire as possible. Hopefully, they'd be drier by morning. With Sven's torso bare, Colette didn't even try to conceal her fascination as she gaped at those intricate scars. She could see Sven watching her from the corner of his eye and didn't miss the subtle flexing of his muscles as he moved about their tiny shelter.

"What are they?" she asked.

"My *idadi*. My people mark ourselves for every kill we make."

The man had dozens and dozens of marks. Glancing away, Colette sucked the last of the coyote fat from her fingers, surprised at how good it tasted. Room and board—all in the same tiny den. It was the only thing to have gone right today. Well, not so much for the former residents. She'd have to wash her bloodied arrows in the morning. Without looking up, she feigned casualty. "What kind of kills?"

"Yeti, imps, blood-seekers." He shrugged. "A variety of things."

Was he being serious? Those were not common prey. Most who'd seen the likes of them didn't live to tell the tale. Suddenly, the idea of victory scars didn't seem so extreme. Still. "Doesn't it hurt like hell?"

Sven snatched up a rock and began digging a hole for the coyote carcass. "We grow accustomed to it."

He was a hard man. That much was obvious. Had so much bloodshed darkened his soul? He was an ass to be sure, but was he also cruel? Colette wrapped an arm around her knees.

"Which marks are for the men you've killed?"

He paused, glancing at her from across the fire. "I haven't killed any men."

"Would you?"

Sven resumed digging. "If I had cause."

"Such as?"

"If I feared death. Mine or that of someone I loved."

Fair enough.

Colette considered everything she'd learned about him today. Before, she'd thought him a domineering brute. Now she *knew* he was a domineering brute who also possessed a gentle side. He'd recognized the danger they were in, acted quickly and decisively. He could have left her behind the moment she'd begun to slow him down. It would have been wiser. Instead, he'd fought her tooth-and-nail, enduring a broken nose and bloodied hand, just to keep her safe. How wholly impressive.

Damn him.

His task complete, Sven scooted around the fire to where she was sitting.

Colette released her legs and stretched her toes toward the flame.

When he was seated right beside her, Sven turned and raised himself onto his knees. Without a word, he swung an arm and a leg over hers and paused so he was crouching directly in her face.

Colette began to stiffen, but the devilish glint twinkling in his gaze compelled her not to give him a reaction. She forced herself not to lean away, and instead stared right back into those dark eyes, arching a brow for good measure. A moment passed, and the crackling of the fire behind him was all she could hear.

He huffed, a rueful grin playing at his lips as he settled himself on her other side, between her and the cave's entrance. "Time for sleep. Do you want to go first again?"

Colette glanced toward the narrow opening. "Do you think we lost the brujit?"

"We can hope."

"I'll stay awake." She paused, thinking of his words to her yesterday. "Since I already had such a refreshing nap today."

Colette caught a flash of something that looked like shame cross his expression as he lay flat next to her. Maybe the barbarian had a conscience after all. Colette wedged a hand on the ground and stared down at him. "Your people, the Dokiri, they don't go to war?"

He tucked his hands beneath his head. "Our war is with the evil that wanders out from under the mountain. Not with other nations. Be grateful. My people keep you lowlanders safe."

"And you think that gives your people the right to take any women they want as wives?"

He gave a firm nod.

In truth, it seemed a reasonable arrangement to her, but she'd not admit that to him. Not in a thousand years. She rolled her eyes. "How primitive."

He chuckled. "As if crudeness really offends *you*."

Colette's brow wrinkled. He spoke so casually. So familiarly. As if they'd known each other for years instead of days. It was strangely intimate and, for some reason, it lent her comfort. This man was starting to get to her. Or maybe it was this place toying with her mind.

Sven tilted his head. "I think you'll like Bedmeg."

He said it like her going there with him was a foregone conclusion. Curiosity outweighed her desire to argue. "Oh? Why's that?"

He reached up to run his fingers down a strand of her hair, making her scalp tingle. "Because it's like you. Fierce as it is beautiful."

"Are you trying to woo me, savage?"

"And if I am?"

His fingers curled around her hair, and he began drawing her head downward.

Colette put up no resistance, following the pull of his hand until she could feel the warmth of his breath gliding across her face. Every nerve in her body fired at once until she was practically alight. Her lips parted even as her lids slid over her eyes. His own eyes narrowed with intensity, his aim plainer than the sun.

At the last moment, Colette stiffened, halting the momentum between them. Her hushed voice came out throaty. "I'd wonder why you bother."

He blinked, his expression morphing from surprise, to defeat, to frustration.

Colette smirked, hiding her own disappointment. After all, he didn't really want *her* per se. Hadn't he said any woman would do? Obviously, passion wasn't high on his priority list. And who did he think *she* was anyway? That she should crumble to his will when he'd offered her nothing in return? Not even a piece of his heart.

A muscle in Sven's jaw worked, but he released his hold on her hair. "Always a battle. Do you ever surrender?"

Colette straightened, flipping her long mane over the opposite shoulder. "Never. And I never lose."

"Your wet clothes disagree."

"Today was a minor skirmish." She glared down at him. "Make no mistake, barbarian, the war is already lost for you."

"Right. I forgot. You've got a fancy nobleman waiting for you."

Colette's stomach tightened at the mention of Lord Myron. In the chaos of the past day, she'd completely forgotten about her impending engagement.

Sven went on, his tone full of mockery. "Let me guess, his father's probably already asked your father if he can maybe, possibly marry you someday. I can't imagine how I'll ever break up that idyllic romance."

The truth of his words struck a little too close to home. Without meaning to, Colette found herself comparing the two men—in particular, the manner in which they'd gone about 'claiming her'.

In total fairness, Lord Myron had been no more concerned about what Colette wanted than Sven. Myron wanted the idea of her, nothing more. Now she thought of it, she'd recently managed to lose further respect for the little lord. In Sven's own absurd way, he was right: having one's father arrange his marriage was more than a little pathetic. And yet, that was the way of Colette's culture. Could she really judge Sven's? She frowned, not liking the direction of her thoughts.

"It doesn't matter what you say. He's in love with me." *That's more than you can say, savage.* "We *will* be together."

From his place on the ground, Sven gave her an unimpressed look. "We'll see."

She stifled the overwhelming urge to strike him. "You'd best get some sleep, barbarian. If I have to, I'll bite your other hand to wake you up."

He grunted, turning away on his side. "I need to teach you some better uses for that pretty mouth."

BY THE TIME she shook Sven awake, the fire had long since burned through its kindling. A bed of warm amber embers let off the only light in the blackened cave. Though Colette's teeth chattered, Sven's bare skin glowed with heat. Did the man never chill? Was he even human? Curse him. She pinched him hard on the arm when he took a little too long to rouse.

"Ow!" he hissed. "Damn it, woman."

She grinned, sorry that he couldn't see her amusement. "G-get up. It's your turn."

She felt around in the dark and cursed when she confirmed her dress was still too damp to wear. Beside her, she heard Sven shuffle to a sitting position and rub at his face with a sigh. She just started to slink down to the ground when he scooped an arm beneath her waist and hoisted her into his lap.

Colette threw her arms to the sides, going completely rigid. "What are you doing?"

"Regna, you're colder than a witch's tit!"

He was warm as bathwater, and felt every bit as divine. Though roughened with scars, the muscled planes of his chest were just soft enough to make her want to lean into him. She barely resisted.

"Let me go, savage, or I'll—"

"Hush. We both know you'll never get to sleep while you're this cold."

Colette pursed her lips. "What? Are you going to hold on to me all night?"

"Yes."

Her face slackened, and her body began to ease. Well then, if he was offering. It wasn't as though this would be the first time she slept in his arms. She probably *would* get to sleep much quicker. Colette forced herself to relax, barely bringing her head back against his chest. He widened his legs so the sides of her body were walled between their warmth. Even laid over him, her toes didn't reach his ankles.

"Are all men built like you where you come from?"

Sven wrapped his arms around her waist, and Colette reminded herself to breathe evenly. "Not all are so impressive."

She scoffed, snuggling into his hold. "Thank the gods. I'm not sure the mountain could stand under the weight of so much ego."

He laughed, and Colette had to smile. Once they got comfortable, she closed her eyes. Under her ear, Sven's heart beat steadily in his chest. With great effort, she concentrated on that rhythmic sound, ignoring the wails and shrieking of the night which had kept her thoroughly terrified earlier. The tension eased out of her body but not from her mind. Just as the night before, she couldn't sleep. Gods, how she needed to.

To her utter dismay, heat bloomed in the back of her eyes. Her jaw tightened. This *couldn't* be happening. Was she about to *cry*? Oh no. Please, no. Not here. Not now. Not in front of *him*. She resisted the urge to rub at her face, to sniffle, to give herself away. Against her considerable will, a warm tear slid past her shut lids and onto Sven's bare chest.

Maybe he hadn't noticed? Silence and stillness made her

hope. Then, he brought a hand up to her head and ran it down the length of her red-blonde mane. Damn him.

"Why do you fear water?"

Colette's eyes popped open, though it was too dark to see. Shame-filled memories came flooding to her mind. It wasn't something she talked about, but then, anything seemed preferable to lying there listening to that bloody forest.

"I told you—I can't swim."

He was quiet, and Colette could feel him waiting for a true answer. With a discreet swipe at her eyes, she sighed. "I almost drowned when I was a girl."

"What happened?"

"My brothers wanted to go for a swim at the lake near our keep. The oldest, Gareth, said they didn't want to mind a babe while they were gone. He told my nurse to keep me from following them."

As he listened, Sven continued to wind locks of her hair around his finger.

Colette focused on the soothing sensation as she spoke. "I managed to get away from my nurse, not that it was any great hardship, mind you. The woman was about a hundred years old and half blind."

"I see you've grown into your defiant streak."

Colette half-smiled, half-grimaced. "I snuck to the lake and made it all the way to the end of the dock before my brothers noticed me. The next thing I knew, they were all shouting and swimming toward me like they were going to thrash me and leave me tied up in my chamber for the rest of the year. So I jumped in."

"How old were you?"

"Four."

Sven muttered something foreign under his breath. "What happened next?"

"I don't really remember much else, just that the water seemed colder than ice and darker than this cave. I've been told Willam got to me first and between the five of them they managed to pump my lungs."

"They must have been terrified."

"Mostly furious." Especially Gareth. At sixteen, he'd blamed himself for what happened and the two of them had butted heads constantly over the years as a result. Other than their mother, Gareth seemed the most determined to make Colette behave herself, which, of course, made her all the more stubborn where he was concerned.

You're not brave, Colette. You're foolhardy. For your own sake, you ought to find someone smarter you're willing to listen to.

I'll let you know if I ever see one, brother.

Despite her flippant dismissal, there was always a part of her that knew he was right. The fact that she was here, trapped in the same forest she'd ridden headlong into, was a testament. Even so, Colette knew marrying her off to Lord Myron wasn't the answer to anyone's problems. She'd crush that man like the little insect he was.

Beneath her, Colette felt the muscles in Sven's chest flex as he switched his "petting" arm. She remembered how tightly those arms had held her in the water, not giving her an inch. Apparently, not all men were so easily vanquished.

"I'm sorry for today," Sven muttered. "I didn't know."

"And if you had?"

"I would have been...kinder."

Yesterday, she would have scoffed at that. Now? Listening to the soft timbre of his voice and lying snugly in his embrace, Colette believed him. Something pleasant unfolded in her chest. Peace. She cleared her throat and curled deeper against his warmth.

"Well, I still would have broken your nose."

7

COLETTE

Colette squinted through the shadows ahead. It was close to midday, and yet the forest was barely brighter than a moonlit night. A cool mist weaved through the trees, amplifying the scent of decay that hung heavy in the air. Beside her, Sven hurried forward and used his axe to clear away the thicket blocking their path. The steel edge tore through scraggly branches, making them quiver and shake like gnat's wings.

Colette's gaze drifted upward toward the bare tree limbs that hung above. She blinked. Had the boughs just moved? Reached toward Sven's shoulders? She rubbed at her eyes then looked again. Everything was in its proper place. For now. Wary, her gaze continued to dart back and forth.

The sudden rumbling of her stomach drew Sven's gaze. "You've an appetite as bad as mine, woman."

She put a hand over her belly. "There's hardly any game in this godsforsaken wood. I'm about to go digging in the dirt for worms. Or perhaps some nuts."

"Don't touch anything that grows here." Sven's eyes flickered to the trees above him, and Colette wondered if he'd been seeing bizarre things, too. "I don't trust it."

Colette said nothing. Of course, she didn't trust it either, but she was also half-starved. They'd walked for hours without spotting so much as a track or scratch. Apparently, animals completely avoided this section of the forest. That explained the deathly quiet. Indeed, the sound of the nearby stream was all that broke up the eerie silence.

Eager for a distraction, she let her thoughts drift to the night before. Had she actually slept neatly tucked in a barbarian's lap? Heat warmed her cheeks at the cozy memory. As they walked, Colette's eyes bored into Sven's broad back. Had he enjoyed it as much as she? She could almost make herself ask him.

"So..." She hesitated. "Any chance we'll reach the forest's edge before nightfall?"

Sven continued to cut the path. "If we're lucky, we might get there the day after tomorrow."

"Oh."

Why was she not muttering a curse or kicking at the dirt? Instead, she found herself staunching the impulse to skip. Sven's news hadn't upset her. In fact, were it not for hunger and for these damned trees, Colette could almost look forward to more time here. Or rather, more time with *Sven*. Had she gone completely insane? She inhaled a waft of blighted fog and decided it was a genuine possibility. She scrubbed a palm over her face.

Give yourself a break, Colette. It's not as if you've some grand destiny waiting for you back home.

They stepped into a narrow clearing, and, for a brief moment, Colette could feel the warmth of the sun caressing her flesh. A felled tree lay just ahead, fractured bits of its rotted stump splintered toward the sky. Sven stepped over the high log, barely avoiding the slick gray moss that covered the bark.

Colette took his offered hand and hopped over the giant obstacle, landing with a thud on the spongy ground. Sven walked on as Colette switched her bow from one shoulder to the other. Just as she was about to follow, something caught her notice.

Maiden's claim. A long patch of the brown, porous mushrooms grew along the crevice between the ground and the fallen tree. Though it was typically dried and ground into powder for its scarlet dye, Colette knew the bitter fungi could also be eaten. She'd had it many times herself. Too bad they had no means to boil it. Still, food was food. She reached out to harvest a handful.

"Get back!" Large hands snatched her by the hips and swung her away.

Colette gasped as a puff of vapor shot from the mushrooms into the air before them. They both threw their heads back, coughing and gagging on the acid stench. Lungs on fire, her eyes burned, water welling up and blurring her sight. Through a wavy haze, she could see Sven bent over, trying to wipe the sticky fluid from his face. He'd taken the brunt of the spray.

Squeezing the tears from her eyes, Colette straightened, fully intending to help Sven. Instead, her head continued its upward trajectory until she was falling completely backwards. She collapsed upon the damp ground with a huff. Colette stared at the spinning, gray canopy above and saw her arms shoot out in front of her, as though looking for something to grab onto. Her fingers closed around empty air. She tried to bring her head up but all she managed was to roll onto her side. The world continued turning even as she locked upon Sven's prone figure.

He was staring at his axe which lay on the ground between them. His reddened gaze drifted over and wavered upon her face. Shame pinched a knot in her stomach. This was probably the part where she should humbly apologize for ignoring his very reasonable instructions.

Her lips parted. "Mistakes were made."

A slow smile spread across his bearded face.

Colette blinked at him and felt herself smiling back.

"You're going to be the death of me, woman." His voice was thick with glee and a round of giggles burst from his throat.

Colette joined in even as his giggles mounted into hysterical laughter. In the back of her mind, she registered that he was being too loud. "Sven, shh!"

He flashed white teeth and extended an open hand in her direction.

Colette's head tipped back. He looked tempting. Unreasonably so. She rolled onto her stomach and crawled over, barely avoiding the axe.

Sven pushed himself to his side and watched her with avid fascination, his pupils taking up most of his eyes. His words slurred past his lips. "*Glanshi*, there's a sight for the gods. You on your hands and knees, crawling my way."

Colette grinned, swaying. Walking her hands up his chest, she shoved him onto his back and wavered over him until her nose hung just over his. "You've got a lot of nerve talking to me like that, barbarian." She giggled. "Why, if my brothers were here, you'd be short a hand or two."

"Ah, but you like it, don't you?" He was practically shouting in her face.

Colette clapped a hand over his chin and slid it up to cover his mouth. "I may. I admit nothing."

Sven fumbled for her wrist, unable to get ahold of the hand she covered his mouth with. Giving up, he batted her arm away. Whatever had drugged them, it was hitting Sven hard.

His voice quieted. "Don't be boring. Tell us the truth. You stripped me down that first day, didn't you? Filled those sultry eyes?"

"What if I did?"

His expression blazed with smug satisfaction. He began

chattering in his language as though she should understand him.

"Speak trade-tongue, Sven."

His head lolled to the side, and his eyes seemed to lose track of her. Colette caught his face between her hands and pulled it back toward her own. His gaze went in and out of focus before he switched back to her language.

"Mmm, I'd say it's only right I take my turn. You know, in the interest of justice."

Colette gasped, her mouth hanging open. She shoved her face in his, accidentally headbutting them both. Neither of them even flinched. "Have you no shame?"

He grinned wickedly. "None whatsoever."

She sat back on her haunches, keeping a hand on his chest for balance. "Not a chance, savage. Get up. We need to move."

He didn't budge, and Colette wondered if he even could. He stared up at her. "You're right. What was I thinking? I don't want to scare you."

"Scare me?"

"You're so young, after all."

Colette glared, her fists tightening on his furs. "I'll wager I'm older than you."

If only by a few months.

"And then there's your fiancé to think of. He'd be furious."

"He doesn't own me!"

"But you're so very in love with *him*."

"The hells I am."

If they'd had any greater priorities, Colette couldn't recall them. Only one thing mattered at the moment and that was shutting her barbarian up. She dragged a leg over Sven's body, her hands gripping his coat to keep from sliding off his waist. Though it'd slowed down, the forest continued to turn around her, and she swayed as her fingers fumbled with the buttons of her riding coat.

Sven watched her with a hawk's intensity. Impressive considering how very swollen his eyes were. As she peeled back the layers of her clothes, Colette dimly heard her mother's voice screeching at her to stop and consider what she was doing. Uncertainty made her hesitate just as the first chill of cool air licked her bared skin. Her gaze floated downward.

The expression on Sven's face immediately banished any and all shame. He looked like a prince on coronation day. Colette's body began burning from the inside out. With a smirk on her face, she pressed her shoulders back and reveled when his eyes widened. He muttered something in his language that she had a distinct impression was wildly complimentary.

"Like what you see, savage?"

Were those her words? Bold as she was, Colette had never considered herself a trollop. When Sven nodded frantically, she decided she could get used to this hat. His hands were twitching at his sides, but he either couldn't or wouldn't bring them up where she knew they itched to be. Licking her lips, she took him by the wrist and drew his hand up to the center of her stomach.

As she expected, his fingertips continued crawling an upward path. Her body shivered, though she couldn't be certain if it was from his touch or the toxin coursing through her. She sighed all the same, basking in the sensation. Instead of stopping to graze the swell of a breast, Sven went on between them and fingered the spot just above her heart.

"Oh, *mu hamma*." His voice was deep and husky. "If I had my knife, I'd mark you right now."

Colette choked on a breath, her face went slack. "What?"

Sven closed his eyes on a contented smile, seemingly oblivious to her sudden alarm. "You're mine. I'll make sure everyone can see. Soon enough."

Colette shoved his hand away and tossed herself off his body, landing hard on her rear. "What in the *swiving hells* are you talking about?"

His eyes still closed, Sven's smile remained. He shifted on the ground as though getting comfortable for sleep.

Colette reared a leg back and kicked him in the side. "Sven!"

He didn't even twitch. Instead, he mumbled in his language, adding at the end, "You'll forgive me...eventually." Then, he began to snore.

Colette stared at him in a lucid daze, sobriety descending upon her like the claws of his cursed wyvern. Mark her? With his knife? *Gods*, was he being serious? Colette thought of the dozens of scars he wore across his own body, and her stomach dropped like a stone. As she snapped the front of her dress closed, one thought screamed above the rest.

Oh hells, no!

Va kreesha.

Sven groaned against the throbbing ache in his head. His eyes cracked open, breaking a seal of sleep. For once, he was grateful for his shadowy surroundings, and, at least, the trees had stopped spinning. He flexed his fingers then hissed. He'd been lying on his axe arm, and the limb was alight with the burn of pins and needles. *Glanshi*.

The smell of damp earth filled his nose and the sound of water running nearby brought Sven's senses to full awareness. Clarity struck him, making him forget his aches and pains. Where was Colette? He threw himself upward, nearly striking the ground between his legs with his head. He pressed a palm to his skull and whipped a glance all around him.

She was there, sitting on the ground across from him. She

looked very much as she had the first time he'd woken in her presence, with her knees drawn up to her chest and her elbows propped against them. Just like that first day, her eyes flashed at him with ominous intent. Despite that look, his shoulders eased.

Safe.

A muscle tightened in his jaw. Was this woman incapable of following even the simplest of instructions? Would it cause her heart to stop cold in her chest? They could have both died while lying here and who knew how many hours they'd lost in the meantime. He swallowed, trying to tamp down his rising anger. They'd survived. That was the important thing.

Colette arched a brow at him. "What did you dream about?"

"Witless women."

"Is that all? Are you sure?"

He scowled, rubbing the blood back into his dormant arm. "Isn't that enough?"

Colette tilted her head with an odd emotion riddled on her face that Sven struggled to name. Mischief? Temper? Embarrassment? Memories began leaking through the rubble of his still-dizzy mind. A pulse of heat warmed his blood. Surely *that* had been a dream.

"Did you..." His gaze fell to her chest.

"Yes?" Her voice was all innocence.

He leaned back on his palms and allowed a knowing smile to slither across his face.

Colette blushed, confirming his sweet recollection. His little storen had flashed her very impressive feathers for him. That explained her dour attitude. Now the danger had passed, Sven could almost be glad for the little delay. He'd never let her live this down.

Serves the she-devil right.

He cocked his head. "Well, I did try to warn you."

"Mmm." She nodded. Though her cheeks were red, her eyes

remained icy cold. "And here I've been thinking you should have warned me about *you*."

Sven shrugged and cast around for his axe. "I do believe that little show was *your* idea. All the more gratifying for me."

"Oh, Sven, I can't imagine you were truly satisfied."

"I assure you, I was."

"Really? Even without a dagger to cut me up?"

Sven's neck stiffened then swung round to where she sat crouching. Her face was plain as a blanket of freshly fallen snow.

Dread crawled up his stiffening spine. "What did I tell you?"

She raised her chin. "Guess."

Kreesha.

He wasn't ready to deal with this. Not right now. He threw his gaze to the side. "Where's my axe?"

She tossed a nonchalant look around the clearing. "I'm not sure I remember."

"Colette, tell me where it is. Now."

Her impassivity slid away like molted scales. "If you think I'm about to lend you steel anywhere but your throat after what you said to me today, you're as crazy as you look."

"Damn it, woman! Haven't you done enough? You're going to get us both killed."

This was not the time or place for this conversation. There was a reason why this subject was addressed early and as quickly as possible between a Dokiri and his bride. Like setting a bone, the worst could be dealt with from the onset, the relationship only improving from there.

Colette jumped to her feet and charged across the clearing to where he was sitting. Arms on her hips, she glared down at him. "Explain yourself, savage."

His instincts told him to stand. The wiser part of his mind told him now was not the time to challenge his little firebrand. Mouth flattening, he stared up at her. "When a Na Dokiri claims a bride, he must make her acceptable to our gods before presenting her to our people. When I claimed you, I'd been prepared to take you to *Amo Tanshi*, the bonding place."

"What exactly does bonding entail?"

"I carve a mark into my chest, over my heart."

She stood perfectly still, her posture tight. "And?"

Time to set the bone.

"And also one over yours."

He could see the wheels of her mind turning, her temper building with each furious spin.

"And if a woman were to refuse?"

He shook his head. "There is no refusing a *Na Dokiri* his bride."

"Of course, because it's your right."

He could imagine how that sounded to a lowlander, but she didn't know what he knew. Hadn't seen what he'd seen. He grimaced, trying to think of how to explain. She didn't give him the chance.

"So your people steal innocent women into the mountains, rip off their clothes, and force a knife into their breasts? Is that about right?"

"It's not like that." *Not* exactly *like that.*

"Then what is it like? Because that's the image you've painted."

He climbed to his feet, relieved she didn't step away. "You're not supposed to hear about it like this."

She dropped her head back, looking him fully in the eye. She was so brave. "You mean not until you've got me at your mercy? *Skies*, Sven, why should I ever trust you?"

"Colette, whatever I said before—"

"What? That you'll carve me up nice and good to make sure everyone knows you own me?"

Sven flinched, his jaw going slack. No. He couldn't truly have said *that*. It wasn't possible. Even so, doubt flickered within him, igniting a firestorm of indignation. "This wouldn't have happened if you had just obeyed me."

"Right. Of course, because gods forbid *your* woman think for herself. Or should I say your chattel?"

Sven raked a hand through his hair. "I'd be happy if you'd think at all. Good gods, Colette, you're as reckless as a child! You don't need a master—you need a keeper."

Hurt flashed across her gray-blue eyes. "Lucky me, if we wed, I could get both, and a husband for good measure. I'm only sorry you'll be stuck with an ignorant child for a bride."

A pang of regret twisted in his gut. This disaster was fast hitting legendary proportions. Could he have handled things any worse? Maybe, if he threw his entire soul into it. *Idiot*. He sighed, hanging his head as he tried to rally his thoughts. "I'm sorry."

"Don't be. Never again. You're right, after all. I think this has been good for both of us. Now you understand what I've been trying to tell you."

"And what's that?"

"There are plenty of other women out there for you to claim. I suggest you alter your plans regarding me. You're not up to the task."

"The hell I'm not."

Before she could blink, Sven closed the distance between them.

8

COLETTE

Sven caught her by the waist and jerked her body against his. Colette's mouth fell open on a gasp of outrage. Was he mad? She started to ask him only to have her words swallowed up by the press of his lips on hers.

Colette's body went totally still, shock stalling all rational thought from her mind. Her savage had her in his arms. A sudden flood of sensation overwhelmed her.

His fingertips drew their way up her sides, the clasp of his hands nearly encircling her entire waist. The stubble of his beard tickled her skin. His body was full of warmth and hard planes. The scent of him was all male, heady and intoxicating. Colette's eyes slid shut. His lips were surprisingly soft yet unyielding as they moved across hers, exploring. One of his hands released her waist only to trail up her spine and press the back of her head forward, further deepening the caress. Colette sighed then shivered as he took her breath into his lungs.

Her first real kiss.

Gods, he felt good. He pulled a hair's breadth away, sucking in air. All at once, she needed to see him, to know if he looked the way she felt. Her eyes cracked hazily open to meet his languid gaze. Colette blinked at him, her skin soaking up his heat even as realization sunk its teeth into her mind.

She jerked away and sent an open palm careening across his handsome face. The resulting slap echoed off the nearby trees. She clutched her palm to her chest, wincing at the sting.

Sven barely flinched, though he gaped at her as if stunned. He shook his head. "I'm sorry. I didn't think—"

"That's for certain." She whirled away, determined to hide her flagellating emotions. What just happened? Why had she let him kiss her? Why had she made him stop? Her body hummed with hot energy. She tugged a hand down her braid, trying to decide what to do. She spun. "Is this it then? You would have me resign myself to your plans for me? Your wishes? To hell with what I want? Just so long as you get your prize?"

"No, that's not it."

"You don't even want me, Sven. I'm simply convenient for you."

"That's not true."

"No? Really? And I'm to believe that after the things you've said?"

He didn't answer. Instead, his gaze snapped toward the trees, away from the creek.

Colette planted her hands on her hips. "Nothing to say?"

He didn't move. "Be quiet."

Was he shushing her? "Are you serious?"

No response.

Enraged, she darted beside the nearby thicket and extricated his axe. With effort, she tossed it on the ground near him. Let him have whatever he wanted then. "Here's your pretty axe."

"Damn it, Colette. Be silent."

She opened her mouth to shout back. Then, she heard it.

A voice, a man's, calling in the distance. *"Colette!"*

She tensed. Was that...her name? She lunged toward the

trees. From the corner of her vision, she saw Sven's arm shooting out to grab her. She sidestepped him, plunging forward.

"Colette!" His voice was thick with urgency, but it remained low, as though he was trying to keep his silence.

Colette ignored him. After a moment, she could hear the thunder of his footfalls behind her. Her back straightened just as his fingers brushed at her spine. Her burst of speed kept her just out of his reach.

He stumbled behind. "Stop!"

She blew past the same scraggly branches that had looked so ominous before. They whipped at her face, slicing her skin as she ran. Had her father come for her? Her brothers? Within minutes, she could be out of this godsforsaken forest. Safe. Sven probably knew that, and he was doing all he could to stop her. She charged through another thicket toward the voice.

Her foot caught on something, a raised tree root, and, suddenly, she was flying to the cold ground. She grunted, barely catching herself with her hands and knees. She threw a glance over her shoulder, desperate to keep out of Sven's reach. The snapping of branches reclaimed her attention to what was right in front of her. An otherworldly noise made the hairs on her neck spike on end.

A deep trilling sent a tremor through her limbs. She raised her eyes to its source. Up. Up.

Dear gods.

Extending an impossibly long and gaunt leg, a horror from Colette's nightmares slunk from the shadows of the trees. It was shaped like a man, but too tall, too thin. Its limbs were sharp and so emaciated, they appeared little more than blood-streaked bone. And yet, somehow, the creature vibrated a raw, primitive strength. What she'd assumed were the branches of trees were actually two sets of twisted horns connected to the skull of some beastly animal. They moved with the monster who wore the skull like a mask, shrouding its features but for the glowing hollows of two ghostly eyes. Brujit.

Colette threw herself back on her haunches and scrambled backward to rise. A row of bleach-white fangs flashed in a macabre grin from beneath the skull's shade. They snapped at her. Like a flash of lightning, it lunged. She didn't even have time to scream.

Something hit the back of her head, folding her forward. A shadow flew over her toward the creature's outstretched claws. Sven roared, axe in hand and swinging upward. The monster's gaze jumped to Sven just as shining steel tore through the fingers of one hand. An unearthly howl exploded from the creature's throat. Colette's hands shot to cover her ears just as the monster's other hand slashed from the opposite side.

"Sven!" Colette's cry was mute in her ears as she watched her savage try and fail to dodge the oncoming swipe. Blood misted the air as Sven's entire body spiraled, sending him to his knees. Before Colette could react, the brujit sprinted away with a shriek, clutching its severed fingers to its chest.

With a cry, Colette lurched forward to where Sven kneeled in the dirt. His axe had landed head end into the dirt, the only thing keeping him upright.

"Sven! Oh, gods." She was gasping, tears of terror streaking down her face. He didn't move, only trembled with his eyes squeezed shut. The front of his hide coat hung open in four raking gashes, blood oozing from each line. Colette clutched his arms and shook him. "Sven, get up! We have to get you away from here."

He began to shiver, a cold sweat already breaking out across his brow.

Colette gripped him like she could tether him to this plane. She lowered her voice, pleading. "Sven?"

His dark eyes cracked open and fixed on her. "Are you hurt?"

She choked on a sob and threw her arms around him. He groaned, and she released him as quickly as she'd grabbed him. His blood now stained the front of her jacket.

"Come on." She climbed to her feet and pulled on his arm, prepared to drag him if that was what it took. "We have to move before you faint."

Bringing one knee up, he wobbled to his feet, using his axe for balance. "I don't faint. Let's go."

He wasn't fine. Couldn't be. There was so much blood. And yet, he plodded on. Colette kept hold of his arm as they went, afraid he would fall. There would be no stopping him if he did, but still, she clung. They followed the sound of water, eventually finding their way back to the creek bank.

"Should we get back in?" Her instincts railed at the very idea. Colette ignored them.

"It's...too late for that," Sven panted.

Colette slowed, turning him toward her. "Let me see."

Wincing, Sven began to shrug out of his coat. Colette helped him, all but ripping the sleeves off his arms. She held her breath as they pulled up his blood-soaked tunic. The air left her lungs in a woosh.

"They're not deep." Relief flooded her senses, making her dizzy. Or was that the blood? She ripped the shirt over his head and wadded it against the claw marks. Sven hissed as she pushed him to the ground and forced pressure against the wounds.

"Gods, Sven, this is all my fault. I'm so sorry."

He looked at her, brows drawn tight. "I should have known it was still following us. I should have warned you they can mimic human voices."

"You saved me."

"Thank Helig."

The truth seemed so obvious now. How could she have been

so blind? He'd jumped between her and death, ready to accept the consequences. He was *anything* but indifferent. She clearly meant more to him than a convenient bride. She shook her head.

"I shouldn't have run from you. I thought—" Her voice cracked. He turned his face from hers, and Colette could see that he felt as responsible for what had happened as she.

"That I was trying to keep you against your will?" Even through teeth that were gritted in pain, he managed an impish smile. "What in our history would make you think such a thing?"

Her heart cracked open and began to ache. How could she have been so foolish? What if he died? What if she had to bury him? The ache turned to a searing throb. No. He wouldn't die. She wouldn't let him. The bastard had promised to get her out of these woods, and she'd be damned if he got out of his oath so easily.

Her chin shot forward. "Sven, you're going to be all right."

"Be easy, *mu hamma*." He brought a clammy palm to her cheek and, despite her anxiety, she leaned into his touch. "I might start to believe you want me to survive."

"Only because killing you is *my* privilege."

"Right."

A smile played at his lips even as hers began to quiver. A hot tear slid down her face. He stroked it away with his thumb.

"*Shh*, Colette. It's well."

Holding pressure on the wounds, Colette resisted the urge to cover his hand with her own. "What are we going to do?"

His expression hardened. "It will come back. We have to destroy it."

"You've done it before, right?"

"With help, and from my wyvern's back."

Colette bit her lip. "How?"

"Only two ways to kill a brujit. Pierce its heart or set it aflame."

"What will happen if we fail?"

"We'll die."

That wasn't what she meant, and he knew it. The look on his face told her he'd say nothing more on the matter, determined not to frighten her further. But hadn't he already told her? The brujit ate its victims. If the legends were true, it did so while they still lived. Colette's toes curled in her boots.

Swallowing, she eased his shirt back. Four angry lines drew across his ribs from one side to the other, slicing through a swath of rune-like scars. Sven was staring hard at her face, likely gauging her reaction.

"It's going to scar." She grimaced, thinking of the wild designs he was so obviously proud of. "Your *idadi*. I think it's ruined."

He shrugged, his expression unconcerned. "It's only flesh, Colette."

Only flesh. Self-recrimination boiled in her gut. Was he so determined to relieve her of guilt? Surely, he cared more than that. She looked him in the eye and opened her mouth to demand he berate her. All at once, a thought struck. Perhaps he *didn't* care. Maybe to him and his people, *all* scars were seen as noble and honorable. Was his culture really so steeped in blood as that? Was his injury inconsequential? Was that how he viewed marking *her* flesh?

A question for later.

Sven reached across the dirt for his axe, seeming much more in touch with himself than he had been just minutes before. "We're running out of time. We have to prepare."

Colette ground her teeth, determination setting into her like ice in winter. "Tell me what to do."

9

COLETTE

Colette shifted her weight against the trunk of the tree, cringing when the branch beneath her creaked.

In the clearing below, Sven's gaze flickered to her hiding spot. He fixed her with another of the same looks he'd been giving her for the past two hours—the one that said, "Don't you dare come out of that tree."

She glared at him. This plan was trash. But it'd been the one he'd insisted on and the best they could come up with.

Colette squeezed the grip of her bow. Three shots. Three opportunities. The sun was setting. If the monster didn't show soon, her chances of a clear target would go down exponentially. She twirled her lit pipe in her hand, resisting the urge to take a drag. An errant puff of smoke was all it would take to give away her position. The last of her stoutweed glowed orange inside, ready to play its part. Eventually.

Come on, you big ugly bastard. Come out where I can see you.

All she could hear was the running of the nearby stream. For once, she was comforted by the deadly silence of this part of the forest. At least they'd know if anything approached.

Colette watched as Sven leaned over the end of his axe,

appearing casual. It had to be a ruse. Meant to calm her, perhaps? Then again, this wasn't the barbarian's first brush with monstrous creatures—though Colette had a hard time imagining worse circumstances. Still, he stood there with inhuman ease, and her admiration continued to grow.

Had she ever met a fiercer male? Not by a long shot. If she were the praying sort, she might have asked the gods for more time. A chance to discover more of him, to reveal more of herself. Were there enough hours in a lifetime?

A branch snapped from several yards away. A rush of adrenaline brought Colette's mind and senses fully to the present.

It was here.

Her body tensed, and she forced herself to breathe as she shouldered her bow and silently withdrew an arrow. Freshly harvested tree sap glistened on the iron point, ready to burn. Not yet. She'd wait for the right shot, just as they'd planned.

Below, Sven remained stooped over his weapon, showing no signs of alarm. Colette winced at the streaks of dried blood on his shredded tunic. Could the beast smell it? Would it be driven mad with temptation? Again, she forced herself to focus, tamping down her fear for Sven. They couldn't afford for her to panic.

Just like hunting mountain lions, Colette. It's just like hunting.

If only the brujit were as stupid as lions. If only she cared so little for the bait.

That familiar deep trilling sounded from somewhere behind her tree. Damn it. She couldn't see. Sven straightened now, his gaze fixing past her. With uncanny calm, he picked up his axe and, without raising it, began to walk away. He kept his eyes on what she could only assume was the monster. So steady. He was luring it, getting it within her line of sight.

Be careful, Sven.

The monster growled low, the noise stationary. It was letting

Sven walk away? Did it suspect a trap? After all, it had set a trap for her.

Colette ground her teeth. She started to inch around the trunk, anxious to know exactly where it was. She stopped herself, remembering how likely she was to give herself away.

For once, Colette, follow the plan.

Sven was coming up against the creek bank now. He slowed, stopped. Waited. Colette's skin tingled all over, her breaths coming in shallow, rapid gasps. Her palms grew slick against the shaft of her arrow.

Calm. It's just a hunt. Just a hunt.

The tree shook, branches snapping like cracks of thunder. She dropped her pipe and arrow in a mad attempt to catch the branch in front of her for balance. The rough bark ripped her nails, but she managed to clutch it with bleeding fingers.

"Colette!"

Her head snapped down, searching for Sven, only to have her vision blocked by the pale swipe of a claw-laden hand. She screamed, throwing herself against the trunk of the tree even as the monster used the branches to swing around and face her.

Glowing eyes locked on her, and an ear-popping shriek blasted from its lipless mouth.

His rancid breath sent hair flying out of her face. Colette tucked her chin and stifled a scream. *I'm going to die!*

The brujit gripped an icy palm against her waist, the span of its fingers spilling over to the tree behind her.

Thunk.

The creature stiffened, shoving the air out of Colette's lungs. It wailed as it slid out of the tree. Colette went with it. Everything was moving too fast. She shoved out her hands, desperate to protect her head. The brujit hit first. The impact forced its limbs loose. The hand that had broken Colette's fall popped open. She rolled across the dirt, her bow somehow remaining

Sven the Collector

intact. Colette sputtered and pushed herself up from the ground.

Now Sven was grappling with the brujit. He went flying into the dirt as the creature flipped over to all fours. Sven's axe protruded from its back, though no blood trickled from the wound. The brujit roared at the sky, and even the trees seemed to cringe away. It spun, trying to reach the axe, tearing divots into the ground with its monstrous feet.

"Colette, the fire!" Sven stumbled up and drew her long hunting knife.

Colette choked on a cry, butfished out her flint and steel and began furiously striking. A sickly sucking sound told her the axe had been removed. Would the creature throw it away? Use it? Should she be dodging even now? Without pausing, she risked a glance up. The axe was flying end over end, straight for Sven's head. He dodged it.

The creature roared.

Her barbarian broke into a run.

No time!

Sparks jumped from the flint. Her pipe was gone. Without hesitation, Colette guided the tiny spits of flame to the end of her red-blonde braid. They caught instantly. In one fluid motion, she threw down the flint and unsheathed her dagger. The braid was severed from her head in the space of a breath. She left it burning in the dirt and shot to her feet.

Only two arrows now. Two chances. She lowered a point into the fire and nearly fainted with relief when it lit up. She brought the bow up to bear and focused on the horrific scene ahead.

The brujit was on top of Sven.

Terror shot through her body, and she released the arrow. The string slapped at her bracer as she watched the shaft zoom over the monster's back.

Oh, gods!

She withdrew the other arrow, set it into the fire. Lining up her final shot, she watched as Sven planted her hunting knife into the hollow of the creature's skull, causing it to rear in pain. She willed herself not to fire. Not yet.

With a roar, the creature came back to the ground and slammed its open hand against Sven's chest. The ground shuddered beneath her feet. Another horrific shriek, this one was inches from Sven's face.

Colette let the bowstring go.

The brujit burst into flame like a dry field in the heat of summer. It screamed, darting forward. Sven went trailing after it like a disjointed marionette, and Colette's blood turned to ice in her veins. Her savage's belt was caught in the creature's stolen horns. They went careening downward, disappearing into the creek bed below.

Colette was halfway across the clearing before she realized what had happened. Sheets of water flew into the air, shrouding her view. Colette might have screamed his name, but she couldn't hear anything over the thundering of her heartbeat. She reached the bank and tried to peer through the walls of splashing water. Even half-submerged, the brujit remained aflame. It spun and bucked, ripping Sven's dangling body this way and that. How long would it take to die? If Sven was moving purposefully, Colette couldn't tell. Her mind spun with horror. What could she do? Her eyes darted for the axe that lay far away.

With a screeching cry, the brujit began to slow. Blood flowed from Sven's temple. His eyes were shut. Colette went numb but for the fear ripping at her insides. She turned, preparing to make a dash for the axe, when the monster suddenly went still. It let out a final pathetic whimper before it collapsed, its massive frame sinking beneath the surface. A limp Sven went down with it.

"No!"

All rational thought fled her mind, replaced by a single, dire purpose. She leapt over the edge. Her feet plunged through the water and bounced off the muddy ground below. With a single stride, she was soaked up to her chin. She could see the brujit's gaunt hip as well as its antler, the wrong one, still cresting the surface. She held her breath and threw herself forward. The tips of her fingers brushed against charred bone. She clung to it, forcing her head beneath the water.

Panic seized her as the icy current rushed overhead. She kicked against the bed of the creek, inhaling a mouth full of water just before she broke the surface. She sputtered, sucking down smoky air. Her fear of the brujit supplanted, she drew her knees up and clambered up its partly submerged body. She couldn't move. Was she paralyzed?

Get him free. Save him.

If she didn't act now, she was going to lose him. *Sven* was going to die. Sucking in a breath, Colette abandoned all sense and dipped below the current. It didn't matter that she couldn't see. The brujit's body was eerily distinct. She followed its limbs to its neck, its neck to its head. With a fierce tug, she withdrew her hunting knife from its eye. Keeping her hand on its skull, she resurfaced for air.

One gulp.

Back down.

She felt for Sven's thick belt, tethered to the creature's twisting horns. Better a wounded side than drowned lungs. Colette hacked at his belt, sawing through the hide. Her chest screamed for air. She ignored it. Determined. The tension vanished and, all at once, the current was pulling her savage's body away from her. She gripped him, then pushed with all her might against the brujit.

Clinging to him, Colette kicked downstream. She kicked

until her legs burned and ached. At last, they were nearing the steep bank. She put her feet down, and was shocked when they reached the bottom. She towed him to the water's edge and hauled his body against it.

"Sven?" Her voice was hoarse and still half-flooded. "Sven, wake up!"

Blood continued to run down his face. He didn't move. She pressed her ear against his chest and could hear nothing over the bubbling of the stream. No. He couldn't be dead.

"Sven!" She balled a fist and struck him against the shoulder. "Get up!"

She screamed, continuing to strike him. Soon, she was unleashing a flurry of blows at him, both of her clenched hands raining down upon him. Tears warmed her cheeks. Was she going mad? Her assault devolved into slamming her entire body's momentum against him, both forearms pounding into his chest.

A gush of water shot past his lips, his entire body curling forward. He hacked.

A startled gasp escaped Colette's throat. In an instant, she was clutching his head, helping him turn to rid his throat of fluid. He clung to her, coughing up all but his teeth. As some of his tension eased, Colette began weeping, smoothing the hair out of his glassy eyes. "You're alive. You're safe."

"Colette?" If possible, his voice was throatier than hers. "The brujit?"

"It's dead. It's dead."

"Are you hurt?"

She shoved her lips against his, kissing him with an urgency that bordered on hysteria. When she pulled away, Sven was gasping for air as though he'd only just awakened. At least the color had returned to his skin. He watched her as though enthralled.

Colette pressed her forehead against his. "I thought you were gone."

Wide eyes blinking, he brought a hand up to her face and stroked at her cheek, as though trying to comfort *her*. She shuddered with relief.

Gradually, Sven's gaze darted around, clarity finally seeming to seep through. "What happened? It came after you in the tree."

"But you stopped it." For once, Colette hoped every bit of her awe for this man shone through. If not, she'd find another way. "You injured it. I set it aflame. That's when our plan fell apart."

"Why are we in the water?"

"Your belt got caught on its mask. It dragged you in trying to escape the flames."

"You—you followed me?"

She nodded. Even the acknowledgment made her stomach sicken with dread. But she'd do it all again. Anything to save him. To keep him.

His lips parted. "But you fear water."

At his incredulous expression, a smile eased across her lips. "Less than some things." Like losing a man she loved, and who so obviously loved her.

"Colette?"

"Yes?"

He quirked a brow. "What happened to your hair?"

10

COLETTE

Two days later.

Colette breathed deeply of the sweet, life-filled air. For the first time in days, unfiltered sun warmed her chilled skin. She turned her face up to it. When she opened her eyes, she caught Sven's wandering gaze on her, his expression inscrutable. Her body tightened as she stared back. What would he do now?

As he'd said he would, he whistled for his wyvern. He'd been convinced it would find them again now that they were free of the forest's oppressive shadow.

"If I were my mount, I wouldn't land here either, even if I could hear my master's call."

Colette waited for him to turn his attention back to her.

"Well, little minx, we survived."

"You sound so surprised."

They'd made it out of the Twist. To her knowledge, almost no one else could make such a claim. Her mother would faint. Colette was ready to. Hunger gnawed at her gut, and she was sure she'd never been so cold in all her life. Thoughts of food and fire consumed her. At the moment, only one thing seemed more important. She cocked a brow at her savage.

He muttered something in his language. "*Shocked* is a better word."

Shifting, she planted a hand on one hip. "Had you known me better, you could have stowed your doubt."

"Indeed."

They stared at one another, their unasked questions stirring between them.

Colette's voice softened. It was low enough to draw him closer. "How will you show me your gratitude?"

"What does a lady want from a savage?"

What didn't she want from him? *With* him? She turned away. A gentle breeze rolled across the grassy hills, across her neighbor's ancestral lands that were so much like her own. Like home. Could she leave it all behind? Her father's voice in her head reminded her that she'd be doing so regardless. No matter what. Footsteps sounded behind her. She didn't tense when she felt Sven's hands at her waist, didn't pull away.

"Come with me, Colette. Be my bride."

She drew in a breath then turned in his arms. His gaze was as steady as his hands upon her, though he didn't move, didn't speak. Only waited.

"What if I refused? Would you force me?"

"Colette, I don't think a man could force anything of one such as you."

A tentative smile quirked at the corner of his mouth, and Colette resisted the urge to return it. She needed answers. He owed her that.

"Would you find another? Someone to suit your purposes?"

His smile faded and hardened into a sober line. "Only one woman will suit me."

He was telling the truth. She knew it. Satisfaction hummed

beneath her skin, making her want to reach out, to cling to him. She settled for brushing a palm against his bearded face.

He leaned into the caress, his voice going husky. "What about you? Could you find happiness with a barbarian?"

She cocked her head as though in deep consideration. "Would I be expected to submit to him?"

"Only in bed." His grip on her waist tightened, sending a thrill of pleasure down to her toes. "And perhaps on very special occasions."

"Like if we're stuck in the wilderness? Being hunted by monsters?"

"Strangely specific, but yes, that might be prudent."

She pursed her lips. "That sounds like utter bondage. I don't know if I can live with it."

He brushed aside a lock of her shorn hair. "I swear to you, he'll find a way to ease your suffering."

"I suppose"—her breath hitched as he pressed his lips to her throat—"with that assurance..."

He drew away, dark eyes searching. "Truly, *mu hamma*?"

She'd since asked him what that term meant.

"There's no word like it in trade-tongue. It roughly means, 'my only'."

A winged shadow glided over them, the call of Sven's wyvern floating down from somewhere within the clouds.

"Yes, Sven. Truly."

EPILOGUE

Two years later

The shrill cry of an infant echoed in the dome-like cave that Sven's people called a *'bok'*. The aroma of woodsmoke, dried leather, and Sven filled Colette's nostrils. Her fingers flexed across the soft hairs of his chest, and she smiled when she felt her husband groan into the furs of their bed.

"I cannot wait until that child is sleeping with the other clan boys."

Colette scoffed. "Just seven or eight more years to go. Bring him to me in the meantime."

With a sigh, Sven rose and edged around the still-glowing fire pit to their son's cradle. She watched him with open amusement. He'd grumbled less to lure the brujit away. She brushed a palm over her sandy eyes. They were both weary and for the very best of reasons.

Outside the caves, she knew an autumn storm raged. Tomorrow, the snow would be waist deep, and she'd once again be amazed at the severe beauty of her mountain home which towered even above the clouds. For now, she drew up the edge of a blanket and rubbed her face against the fibers. How good it felt.

Sven returned with a wriggling bundle in his arms.

Colette collapsed back on the furs, extending her arms in eager anticipation. A wry grin formed at the corner of her savage's lips as he neatly tucked their dark-haired child against her bosom.

The babe wailed, impatient to feed.

"Hush now. Hush, my little Hollen." She'd named their son after her youngest brother, her most willing partner in crime. Colette had wanted to go back, to explain her fate to her family. Reason, however, had dictated otherwise. She couldn't risk the chance that her brothers would come after her, putting their lives at risk. It had been a sacrifice, but one she didn't dwell on. She could only hope her family had found as much contentment as she.

Sven helped her unthread the ties of her gown and guided their son's downy head to her breast. In seconds, Hollen was latched on, tiny suckling noises replacing his cries.

Sven sat at the edge of the bed. He ran a hand over Hollen's hair, the span of his hand draping over the child's little skull. Colette watched him, reveling in the comfort of this moment. As the minutes passed, Sven's fingers trailed over to Colette's chest, tracing along the outline of her bonding mark, the one he'd put there.

Her stomach fluttered, recalling that day. For most women, the bonding rite was a terrifying ritual. For Colette, it had been anything but. A familiar heat began pooling in her belly, rising to her cheeks.

When Hollen finally relaxed, his little lips popping away from her breast, Sven scooped him up and took him back to bed. Colette didn't bother to re-lace her shift. As he returned, Sven eyed his pillow like a starving man eyed bread. Colette pursed her lips in mock sympathy.

Too bad.

The second his back touched the blankets, she was upon him. Sven threw his head backward as she rained kisses across his broad chest.

"Ah, Regna, woman, are you never satisfied?"

Despite his protests, his body responded to hers with well-trained enthusiasm.

Colette paused her ministrations long enough to smirk up at him. "And here I thought you were supposed to be the wild one."

"There's wild and then there's feral. You, my little hell-cat, are the latter."

Just for that, she scratched a path down his well-formed shoulders. He shuddered, barely stifling a groan of pleasure.

"Very well then." He sighed. "Sleep is for the weak."

"*Mmm.* That's my brave savage."

An hour later, they lay side by side, chests heaving. Colette brushed a hand across her dampened brow and chuckled with sheer joy.

No regrets. Never.

Rolling, she swung a leg over her husband's hips, tucking herself snugly against his side. He wrapped an arm around her and used the other to smooth out her hair. Sighing, she began her favorite game of counting his ever-growing collection of scars. It wasn't long before she was keeping track with her lips instead of her fingers. When she hoisted herself over his waist, Sven shook his head, a helpless laugh rumbling in his throat.

"You're going to be the death of me, woman."

The End.

THE DOKIRI BRIDES SERIES

Available Now

Hollen the Soulless
Erik the Tempered
Ivan the Bold

Coming Soon

Magnus the Vast
Sigvard the Nameless

ABOUT THE AUTHOR

When Denali Day was trying to figure out "what to be when she grew up" she noticed all her written stories featured a scene where the beautiful heroine patched up the wounds of a gallant hero. So she decided to become a nurse. Twelve years and two degrees later, she realized all she ever really wanted was to be a writer.

Now she lives in the midwest with her adoring husband, a real life gallant hero, and their two wicked goblins (children). When she isn't writing she's reading and when she's not doing either of those things she's probably plundering the fridge for something she can smother in whipped cream.

www.denaliday.com

ACKNOWLEDGMENTS

While this wasn't the first book I've ever written, it's the first I've ever put out to the public. The year surrounding its publication has been the most trying and incredible time of my life as a writer. Of course I've had significant help from people who want nothing more from me than to see me succeed. Each of them is worth their weight in gold.

AJ, my husband, I doubt there is a better model for that of the "supportive lover". You've helped me in so many ways I could take up a chapter mentioning them. Paramount among them has been your steadfast commitment to seeing me achieve my goals if for no other reason than my own happiness. You've made countless sacrifices on that altar and I'll always be grateful.

Hollee Mands, my critique partner, I'm convinced God put you in my path right from the beginning of this journey by design. I honestly don't know if I would have made it this far apart from your constant encouragement and willingness to come alongside me every step of the way. Thank you for being a friend as much as a teacher.

Kelley Luna, my unofficial editor in chief (and also cheerleader), your enthusiasm cannot be matched. Your joy is infectious and was occasionally the only thing that kept me from hating my work and everything about it. Thank you for puffing up my ego while still managing to teach me how quotation marks work.

Janelle Chapman Brown, occasionally you've supplied me with some of the most creative solutions to story problems I've had and it blows my mind. Thank you for your "outside the box" thinking.

Justena White, if there's an award for fastest reader on the planet, I think you should apply. Thanks for always being an instant message away.

> Philippians 4:13 I can do all things through Christ who strengthens me.

Printed in Great Britain
by Amazon